THE DATING GAME

by

Jay Northcote

Copyright

Cover artist: Garrett Leigh

Editor: Sue Adams

The Dating Game © 2014 Jay Northcote

brief quotations embodied in critical articles and reviews.

WARNING

This book contains material that maybe offensive to some and is intended for a mature, adult audience. It contains graphic language, explicit sexual content and adult situations.

Chapter One

Owen stiffened as he caught sight of a tall blond man coming through the door of the bar. The man looked around expectantly and Owen stared in disbelief. It couldn't be…. Bloody hell, it *was*.

"Hey, Nathan! Over here, mate." Owen's friend Simon waved at the newcomer who grinned widely as he approached.

Simon stood to greet Nathan, pulling him into a hug. "Welcome back to Bristol."

"Cheers," Nathan replied. "It feels like coming home."

"This is my boyfriend, Jack." Simon gestured to the man beside him.

Jack waved. "Hi. Good to meet you, Nathan."

"You too."

"And you remember Owen?"

4

Simon's words snapped Owen out of his shocked state, reminding him to observe the usual social conventions and attempt a smile instead of gaping like a dead fish.

Owen reached over the table, narrowly avoiding a pint glass with his elbow, and offered his hand to Nathan to shake.

"Of course." Nathan's pale blue eyes met Owen's, and there was a spark of something — interest or amusement? His grip was strong, and Owen missed the warm clasp of it when Nathan released his hand.

"Good to see you again," Owen said. "Are you back visiting for the weekend?"

"No. I'm here for good." Nathan smiled. "I just started a permanent job with the Environment Agency. Anyway… I need to go to the bar. Anyone else need a drink while I'm there?"

Owen looked at the couple of inches left in the bottom of his pint glass and decided he definitely needed more alcohol to deal with Nathan being back in town.

"Yeah, a pint of lager, please."

As soon as Nathan had gone to the bar, Owen leaned across the table and fixed Simon with a furious glare.

"Why the fuck didn't you tell me?" he hissed.

"What?" Simon tried, and failed, to look innocent. "I guess I forgot. You didn't know him that well, did you? I didn't think you'd be interested."

Jack was frowning and looking between the two of them, obviously trying to work out what was going on.

"Yeah, right. I've only had crush on him for pretty much forever. Of course I'd be bloody interested to know he was back in town." Owen picked up his pint and gulped down the remainder.

"Yeah." Simon chuckled. "Okay, I knew. I just couldn't pass up the opportunity to see your face when he walked through the door." He turned to Jack. "It was an unrequited crush. Nathan was totally straight when we were students."

"Wait. What?" Owen snapped his head back up and met Simon's amused gaze. "You said 'was.' Was totally straight."

"Oh, did I forget to mention that part too? Yeah. He came out last year while he was living in London. Changed his 'interested in' on Facebook." Simon used his fingers to illustrate the quotes.

"Fuck." Owen's brain wasn't ready to accommodate this new information. "Oh bollocks, he's coming back. You're such a wanker for not telling me this before."

Simon was busy trying to stifle his giggles as Nathan walked back toward them with a tray of drinks, so Owen addressed Jack instead. "Your boyfriend is an evil little shit."

Jack shrugged and put an arm around Simon's narrow shoulders, drawing him close and nuzzling the angelic golden brown curls, which belied Simon's penchant for mischief. "Yeah. But he's *my* evil little shit, aren't you babe?"

Owen rolled his eyes as Simon turned to kiss Jack briefly on the lips and they gazed adoringly at each other.

7

"Save me from their nauseating domestic bliss," he appealed to Nathan as he took the seat beside Owen. "I have to live with this at home, and now I can't even escape it in the pub."

"Here." Nathan passed Owen his new drink. "So you live with these guys?"

"Yep. Me and Simon carried on sharing after we graduated, and Jack moved in a few months ago."

Owen had lived with Simon ever since their first year at uni when they were allocated rooms in the same student accommodation. They'd hit it off right from the start and had been best mates ever since.

Nathan had always been part of their wider circle of friends. He'd been doing the same course as Simon, so they occasionally ended up at the same parties or as part of a large group in the student union bar. Nathan wasn't much of party boy, though, and on the rare occasions he'd been out drinking with them, he'd been quiet—not the centre of attention like Owen and Simon often were. But Owen had noticed him all the same and had indulged himself in his straight-boy crush, entertaining what he'd presumed were wild fantasies of turning Nathan, showing him how great it could be with a guy. Apparently someone else had beaten him to it.

Of course Owen had never tried anything because he thought it would be a waste of time. So he'd kept himself busy, fucking his way through a string of different guys, experimenting, having fun, but never falling for anyone. He left uni considerably more sexually experienced than when he began, with a well-deserved reputation for being a bit of a tart—albeit a lovable one.

Owen's gaze dropped to Nathan's large hand where it curled loosely around his glass. His fingers were long, and the golden hair that sprinkled his wrist and the backs of his hands glinted in the overhead light. Owen realised he was staring when Jack broke the silence.

"So, Nathan. Where are you living?"

"I've moved into a shared flat with Kirsty. You'd know her, I think, Owen? She studied Biology with you."

"Oh, yes." Owen nodded, picturing a tall girl with long red hair. "Yes, I remember her."

"Her old flatmate just left to start a PhD in Cardiff, so she had a room spare. It's in Redland."

"Nice," Simon replied. "We're in Montpelier still, in the same place we lived during our third year."

The conversation carried on for a while, moving on to discuss other mutual friends and acquaintances and what they were doing now. Many of them had initially stayed in Bristol after graduation but were starting to drift away as better jobs came up in other cities.

Owen was unusually quiet, still struggling to digest the news that Nathan was gay now. Gay and out. Thinking back, Owen never remembered him having a girlfriend while they were students. He wondered whether Nathan had been celibate or just discreet about any same-sex experimentation.

As the evening progressed, their group got bigger. Other people arrived, more than could fit around their table, and the group split up a little. Some people stood in twos and threes chatting, and a few drifted off to the dance floor at the back of the room.

Owen went to dance for a while, needing to burn off some of the nervous energy that was fizzing through him at seeing Nathan again. When he came back, he found Simon standing at the bar waiting to be served — their places at the table were now taken by a couple of girls chatting with Jack and Nathan.

"Hey." Owen squeezed in beside Simon. "Can you get me another beer if you're being served?"

"Sure."

Once they had their drinks, they stayed near the bar, leaning against the wall.

"Is that Kirsty?" Owen looked more closely at the girls talking to Nathan and Jack. "Wow. I didn't recognise her with short hair. It looks good."

Kirsty's previously shoulder-length red hair was now short and spiky, showing off the length of her neck and her fine features. She looked like a beautiful boy.

"Yeah. It suits her," Simon agreed.

Owen's gaze drifted to Nathan and stuck there. Nathan looked as good as ever. His blond hair was cut in the same short style he'd had at uni, clipped close to his head around his ears and at the back but a little longer and thicker on top. Owen stared longingly at Nathan's tall frame and broad shoulders and imagined what he'd look like with less clothes on. All that deliciously pale skin that flushed so easily. Owen bet it would be really easy to suck marks onto him, and he'd love to find out if he was right.

Simon nudged Owen. "Eye fuck him a little harder, and he won't be able to walk without wincing tomorrow. You're practically drooling. Why don't you go and talk to him?"

"I'm going to." Owen turned his attention back to Simon. "I'm biding my time."

"You gonna see if he wants to hook up, or go out sometime, or what?"

"I guess." Owen took a sip of his beer. "I might as well be upfront about it."

Owen's usual strategy with picking up guys was the unsubtle approach. He'd never bothered with dating, preferring to be frank about his attraction and making it clear it was sex he was after. It rarely failed him. His dark, intense looks and leanly muscled body appealed to lots of guys. He didn't often get turned down once he'd set his sights on someone.

Owen got his chance a little later in the evening. The others were dancing, and Owen was sitting with Nathan and Kirsty. When Kirsty wandered off in search of the toilet, Owen moved his chair a little closer and grinned at Nathan, who smiled back warily.

"So," Owen began. "I gather you're into cock now?"

Nathan's eyes widened, and his cheeks flushed pink. "Um…. Yes?"

"Cool. So, do you wanna get out of here and go someplace to fuck, or suck, or whatever?"

Nathan raised his eyebrows. "Seriously?"

"Yeah." Owen let his gaze slide down over Nathan's torso to land on his crotch. It looked like Nathan might be getting a little hard. Either that, or he was a shower rather than a grower. "I always thought you were hot. I just never knew you swung my way. So how about it?"

Nathan cleared his throat and shifted uncomfortably in his seat. He was definitely getting hard. Owen lifted his eyes expecting to see a smile. But Nathan was frowning and biting his lip.

"That's flattering, but I'm not interested."

Owen raised an eyebrow and glanced briefly at the bulge in Nathan's jeans again. "You sure about that?"

Nathan's face was even pinker now, but he held Owen's gaze. "I'm not interested in a hookup. I've been there, done that, and decided casual sex isn't for me. I'm looking for something more serious."

Owen blinked. This wasn't how the conversation was supposed to go. He found himself blurting out his next words without

14

thinking. "What, like a relationship? I could have a relationship. With you, I mean."

Nathan chuckled then, a snort of laughter that raised Owen's hackles, because what the fuck? He'd made a move and was being laughed at. That wasn't cool.

"What's so fucking funny?"

"Sorry." Nathan pulled himself together and pasted on a more serious expression. "But Owen, you don't *do* relationships. Everyone knows that. I know what you were like at uni, and from what I've heard on the grapevine, you haven't changed much. And that's fine—each to their own. But I don't want to be another notch on your bedpost. I'd rather be friends with you than one of your conquests."

Owen's irritation rose, and he resisted the urge to pout childishly, but he wasn't prepared to back down. Nathan's words had stung, because yes— Owen would be the first to admit he was a bit of a tart on the surface, but at least he was honest about it. He'd never strung anyone along or made promises he couldn't keep. And he'd never met anyone who made him want more than a one-night stand or a few casual no-strings repeats.

But that didn't mean he wasn't capable of having a relationship, and he found himself wanting to prove to Nathan that he wasn't as bad as his reputation seemed to imply.

"Will you go on a date with me instead, then?" he asked.

"A date?" Nathan narrowed his eyes. "What, so we eat first and then have sex? I'm not sure that would be any better."

"We don't have to have *sex*!" Owen protested, raising his voice in frustration, then lowering it quickly as he noticed a few people glancing their way. "Jesus. Contrary to popular opinion, that's not the only thing I'm interested in."

"So if we went on a date, you wouldn't expect me to put out?" Nathan's lips quirked in amusement. He seemed to be enjoying this conversation a little too much.

"Not unless you wanted to."

"I'd like to get to know you better first. I think we'd need more than one date for that."

"Okay, so what's your magic number? Try me."

Nathan's brow furrowed as he considered the question for a moment.

"Five," he finally said. "Five sex-free dates. Then when we've had a chance to connect, we can take it from there. Oh… and in case it wasn't obvious, if this is going to be a relationship, I'd expect you to be exclusive." Nathan sat back in his seat and folded his arms. "So, what do you say?"

Owen glared at him. Nathan's pink lips stretched further as he grinned, and all Owen could think was how he wanted to come all over Nathan's smug face.

"I'm in."

Nathan's smile vanished abruptly. "You're… what, really?"

"Really." Owen smirked, finding Nathan's obvious surprise very satisfying. "Five dates with no sex. So, when are you free this week? I can see you every night apart from Thursday, so if you're free to meet most nights we can be done with all five dates by next weekend."

17

"Oh no. No way." Nathan shook his head. "If we're going to take things slow, the dates need to be spread out. One a week for five weeks."

Somehow Owen had thought his loophole was too good to be true.

"You drive a hard bargain, but okay." He shrugged, conceding some ground, but not defeated. "Next weekend for our first date then?"

"Okay."

"And while we're discussing ground rules for this... whatever-the-fuck this is." Owen waved his hand disparagingly. "What are we counting as sex for the no-sex rule? No fucking obviously, but does that extend to no blowing each other? No handjobs? What about dry humping?"

"Shh!" Nathan's face was flaming, and he moved his chair closer, leaning in so he could talk quietly. "Keep it down, for fuck's sake."

To be fair, Owen's voice had got rather loud, and a group of girls at the next table were looking very interested in their conversation.

"Well?" Owen asked. "We need to be clear what the boundaries are. Can we even kiss?"

"Kissing is fine," Nathan replied promptly, and his gaze dropped to Owen's mouth. He paused before adding, "No orgasms. That's the line."

"No orgasms while we're together, I hope you mean. Please tell me I'm still allowed to wank, otherwise my balls might explode."

Nathan snorted. "Yeah, because obviously that's a physical possibility. But yes. Of course you can still wank, you idiot."

"Even if I think about you while I do it?" Owen grinned, enjoying the blush that coloured Nathan's cheeks at the question.

"Whatever floats your boat."

"Okay." Owen rubbed his hands together. "So we're really going to do this then? First date next weekend? You'd better give me your number, so we can sort out when and where."

They swapped phones and entered their contact details. When Nathan handed Owen's phone back, Owen sent a smiley face to test he had it right. Nathan sent back one with its tongue hanging out.

"That's what you'll look like after five dates with me, baby," Owen teased. "You'll be gagging for it. Just you wait."

Nathan shrugged, amused. "Probably. But by then, sex with you might mean something, and I'd rather wait and find out."

"I bet you were one of those kids who always saved up their Easter chocolate and still had some left at Christmas, weren't you?"

"Well... maybe not Christmas. But I sometimes made it last for a couple of months."

Nathan didn't even sound as though he were joking. Owen just had to hope that Nathan was going to prove more susceptible to his charms than he was to the lure of chocolate, because he didn't want to have to wait five weeks to get into Nathan's pants.

Owen put his phone back in his pocket. "I'll text you during the week, and we'll sort something out."

"Okay."

When they got home after the pub, Owen explained the situation to Simon and Jack. Jack listened sympathetically, while Simon cackled like a hyena on speed.

"I can't believe he got you to agree to it." Simon finally stopped laughing long enough to get a sentence out. "God. You must really like him. You've basically agreed to woo him, like some fucking Victorian suitor or something."

"I bloody haven't," Owen snapped. He clutched his glass of water more tightly and wondered whether he should take some paracetamol for the beer headache that was already making his brain throb. He was going to feel like crap in the morning. "There will be no wooing. We're just going on a few dates to get to know each other. It's not such a radical idea, is it?"

"It's radical for you. You've never been on a date in your life!"

"I have. I went on a date with Lucy Hicks when I was in year ten at school—three dates, in fact."

21

The third date had ended with a fumbled attempt at fingering and had confirmed Owen's suspicions that girl parts weren't his cup of tea. He'd broken it off after that and started swapping blowjobs with Rob from drama club instead.

"So you're going to do it, then?" Jack asked. He appeared to be taking Owen's situation a little more seriously than Simon was, and Owen was grateful.

"Well… yeah. I guess." Owen shrugged. "I do like him. I'm not sure what I was thinking, agreeing to his conditions, but I've done it now, and I'm not one to back down from a challenge. It's only five weeks. How hard can it be?"

Simon giggled. "Very *hard*, I imagine."

Owen glared.

"But maybe the sex will be all the better at the end of it?" Jack suggested. He and Simon were lying back on the sofa, snuggled together like puppies, all sleepy and affectionate.

"Maybe."

Owen wasn't convinced. He thought sex was pretty great even when it was with people he didn't give a shit about. It felt good, he got off, they got off. What wasn't to like about it? Okay, so Simon claimed that sex with Jack was the best sex he'd ever had and liked to wax lyrical about emotional connection, and trust, and shit. Owen found it hard to believe it made much difference. But as he watched Jack tighten his arms around Simon, while Simon idly took Jack's hand and played with his fingers, Owen though that kind of easy intimacy with another person must be nice. Maybe he'd get to find out.

"So where are you going on your first date?" Simon asked.

"I don't know. We haven't discussed it yet. We swapped numbers, so I'll give him a call during the week."

"Playing it cool, are you?" Simon grinned. "Bit late for that, isn't it?"

Owen shrugged. "Whatever. He made me agree to this. I'm not rushing to organise anything for next weekend. I'll leave it a few days before I make contact."

Owen forced down the rest of his water. His belly was full of beer, but he knew he'd be glad he'd drunk the water in the morning. "I'm going to bed now." He put his glass down on the coffee table and pushed himself up from his armchair a little unsteadily. "'Night."

"Goodnight," they replied in unison.

Owen heard whispers and muffled giggles, then the sound of kissing as he closed the door behind him. "No fucking on the sofa," he called back. "Go to bed!"

Owen had only caught them doing that once, but he was determined they'd never live it down.

Chapter Two

"You and Owen were looking pretty cosy last night," Kirsty remarked as Nathan took a seat beside her on the sofa. She muted the TV and turned to face him, tucking her legs up underneath her.

"I suppose," Nathan replied. He wasn't sure he was ready to discuss the events of the night before. He still couldn't quite believe the situation he'd landed himself in.

But Kirsty wasn't going to drop it. "So?"

"I think we're going on a date. Next weekend."

"A date? I didn't think Owen was the dating type. Not from what I've heard, anyway."

"He's not usually," Nathan admitted. "But he wanted to hook up and I told him I wasn't interested in that. Somehow he ended up agreeing to go on dates with me instead."

"Dates, plural?" Kirsty raised her eyebrows.

Nathan nodded. "Five of them."

Once Nathan had finished reluctantly explaining the details of his arrangement with Owen—Kirsty was relentless in her questioning, so he didn't get to leave anything out—he was hot with embarrassment and Kirsty was grinning like it was the best thing she'd ever heard.

"This is hilarious. So Owen has to take you on five dates and impress you with his boyfriend potential before you're prepared to do the dirty with him? And he agreed to this?"

"Basically, yes. I have no idea why."

Nathan didn't get it. He'd thought Owen was kidding at first when he suggested dating, so his challenge of five sexless dates was more of a joke than anything else. He'd fully expected Owen to laugh and then bugger off.

Kirsty frowned thoughtfully. "Maybe he really likes you."

"Or maybe he's a spoilt brat who's used to getting what he wants." Nathan shrugged.

"Well, I guess you'll find out soon enough."

"Unless he wakes up this morning and wonders what the hell he was thinking."

Nathan figured that was likely. Owen could get almost anyone he wanted with his looks and charm. Why would he bother holding out for Nathan?

Nathan had admired Owen from afar when they were at uni. Owen was the sort of person who was hard to ignore. Even if Nathan hadn't had a confusing—at the time—crush on him, he'd have been aware of Owen in his social circle. Striking, sure of himself, and invariably the centre of attention, Owen had fascinated Nathan, who wasn't any of those things. At first Nathan thought he was interested in Owen because he admired him—his confidence, his openness, his easy admission of his sexuality—but later Nathan had to admit there was attraction there too. As Nathan began to accept he was more interested in men than women, Owen was always there on the periphery, gorgeous and tempting but also intimidating. Nathan wasn't ready to go there, so he kept his distance and ignored his feelings.

"Nathan?" Kirsty nudged him with her foot, and he realised he'd drifted off while she was still trying to talk to him. "You okay there? You don't have to go through with this if you don't want to. It was just some drunken bet... well, not a bet exactly, but you know what I mean. If you don't want to date Owen, just text him and tell him."

"No," Nathan replied quickly. "No. I want to try it. I want to give him a chance. I always had a bit of a thing for him when we were students," he admitted.

Kirsty smiled, not looking particularly surprised at this titbit of information. "Aw, that's sweet. And now you get to date your crush, after all this time."

Nathan flushed. "It's not that big a deal." Maybe if he said it out loud he'd be able to convince himself it was true. "Plus it was my stupid idea, so it would be rude to back out now. I made the challenge, and he accepted. The ball's in his court."

"And do you think you can resist his legendary charms for five whole dates when you already fancy him? I can't see Owen being awfully patient. He strikes me as being an instant-gratification sort of man."

"I'm sure I'll cope."

But Nathan had to admit he was worried about that. He was fully expecting Owen to push the boundaries to their limits, and Nathan wasn't sure of his own commitment to the celibacy clause. Yes, he didn't want a one-night stand. But damn it, he'd wanted Owen for a long time.

This was going to be hard — in more ways than one.

By Thursday, Nathan had almost given up watching his phone.

He'd been on tenterhooks ever since the weekend. He kept telling himself it was too soon, and Owen wouldn't be in touch that quickly. But he couldn't stop his heart from leaping every time anyone else texted him.

Then as the days passed, Nathan started to wonder whether Owen had changed his mind. Maybe he'd thought better of their stupid plan.

On Thursday afternoon, Nathan's phone finally chimed with a message.

U still up for our hot date this weekend?

Nathan forced himself to wait an hour before replying. Petty maybe, but Owen had made him wait five bloody days, so Nathan thought he was entitled to make him sweat a little.

Sure, where and when?

He grinned as his phone rang. Taking personal calls at work wasn't generally encouraged, but fuck it. His boss's door was shut, and none of his colleagues would mind as long as he kept it short.

"Hi, Owen."

"Hi. How are you?"

"Good, thanks. You?"

"Yeah. Not bad," Owen replied. There was a short pause. "I thought it might be easier to make plans for the weekend this way. So when are you free, and what do you fancy doing?"

"Ummmm." Nathan drew the sound out, stalling for a moment while his mind raced with the pros and cons of various options. "Saturday afternoon's good for me. How about we just meet for coffee this time?" He thought something low-key would be good.

"Okay. Anywhere you have in mind?"

"How about Cafe Jive near the Arches?" Nathan suggested. It was good and wasn't too far from where either of them lived.

"Is that the one a few doors up from The Red Lion?"

"Yeah."

"What time?" Owen asked.

"Two thirty?"

"Okay. I guess I'll see you then."

"I guess you will. Bye, Owen."

"Bye."

Nathan went back to work with a smile on his face. If any of his colleagues noticed, they didn't comment.

On Saturday afternoon, Nathan was feeling nervous — and annoyed with himself because of it.

"For fuck's sake, Nathan, you're not some blushing virgin, so why are acting like one?" he muttered as he shoved a rejected garment back into his wardrobe. A shirt was too formal, and it would look as though he was trying too hard.

He stomped over to his chest of drawers, pulled out a pile of neatly folded T-shirts, and laid a couple of them out on his bed, trying to decide which looked best with the pale gray chinos he'd picked out first. He picked a dark red one. It would do, he decided.

In the shower Nathan let his mind drift to Owen, his cock thickening in his hand as he washed himself. But he didn't have time for a wank now, or he'd be late. That was bad planning, especially as Owen was likely to be in full-on flirt mode.

When he was dressed and ready to go, Nathan took a final look in the mirror on his wardrobe door. He fiddled with his hair, combing his fingers through the blond waves, and let his eyes drift over the rest of him. He looked fine, casual and comfortable—he knew his arse looked good in these chinos, and he had a feeling Owen would appreciate it.

Owen was already sitting at a corner table by the window when Nathan arrived, a carefully planned few minutes late. The smile of welcome that spread across Owen's face made Nathan's stomach flip. He grinned back, cautiously easing his large frame through the tight spaces between the tables and chairs till he reached Owen.

"Hey," Nathan said.

"Hi," Owen replied, and Nathan tried not to fidget as Owen's gaze raked over him. When he made it back up to Nathan's eyes, Owen cleared his throat. "So… um, can I get you a coffee or something?"

"It's okay, I'll go and order," Nathan offered. "I'm already up. You keep the table. What do you want?"

"A gingerbread latte please."

"Anything to eat?"

"No, thanks, I only just had lunch."

Nathan ordered their drinks at the counter, the latte for Owen and orange juice for himself. When he caught sight of some giant slabs of chocolate brownie, he decided to get one of those too.

He carried his order back on a tray and squeezed into the seat opposite Owen. Cafe Jive was popular, and the owners obviously wanted to make use of every available square inch of floor space, so the tables were crammed in close together. Their table for two was tiny, so once Nathan was settled, their knees touched under the table. But Nathan wasn't complaining.

"Thanks." Owen took his latte and stirred it, then licked the foam off the spoon suggestively.

Nathan watched the flick of Owen's tongue, and his mind went to dirty places. That was obviously Owen's intention, because he smirked when he caught Nathan looking.

Nathan's cheeks heated, and he turned his attention to the brownie. He left the plate in the middle of the table but broke off a chunk for himself.

"Help yourself if you want some. I bought it for sharing." He bit off a piece and chewed.

Owen dug in his pocket for some change. "Here, let me give you some cash for my coffee." He slid a couple of pound coins across the table towards Nathan.

"Don't be daft." Nathan pushed them back. "If we're going on five dates, I'm sure it will even up eventually."

"Okay. I'll get the next round." Owen grinned, and Nathan lost himself in his dark brown eyes until the brush of Owen's leg shifting against his distracted him.

They sat in awkward silence for a moment. Nathan's belly felt fluttery with nerves, and he reached for another piece of brownie to give him something to do. Owen apparently had the same idea, and their fingers bumped. That broke the tension as they both chuckled.

"This feels weird," Owen said. "As you know, I'm not used to doing the date thing. I'm sorry if I'm crap at it."

"I haven't done much of it either," Nathan admitted.

"So…" Owen flicked a strand of dark hair out of his eyes. "We have some catching up to do. Let's start there. What have you been doing since we graduated?"

"Well, I didn't have a permanent job lined up, so I moved back home at first." Nathan paused to eat a chunk of brownie, then continued. "I started off temping, then got a job as a lab technician in a school. I did that for a year until I finally got this job back in Bristol. So, how about you? You've been in Bristol the whole time, yes?"

Owen nodded. "Yeah. I stayed in the house with Simon because I had a job to start straight away."

"What is it you do again?"

"I'm a sales rep for a pharmaceutical company."

"That makes sense."

"What?" Owen frowned.

"You, being a salesman. I can imagine you using your powers of persuasion."

Owen chuckled. "Ah, yeah. I suppose it suits me. All the driving is a pain in the arse, though, but at least I get a company car."

"Really?" Nathan was impressed. He didn't have a car of his own. He couldn't justify the running costs on his salary with the rent he was paying, plus he could easily cycle or walk to work anyway. "What have you got?"

"A VW Golf."

Nathan nodded. "Sweet."

"I'm not very into cars, but it is nice to drive. Pretty smooth. Better than my mam's old banger of a Beetle I learned in."

"Oh, but Beetles are cool. I love classic cars." Nathan leaned forwards, enthusiastic. "When I eventually get around to getting a car myself, I want to get a classic like a Beetle or maybe an old Mini. I'd like to buy an old knackered one and do it up myself."

"I can't imagine you in a Mini." Owen chuckled, his gaze scanning Nathan's frame. "Would you fit? They're hardly designed for blokes your size. Your head would be jammed against the roof, surely?"

Nathan laughed. "Maybe. I don't know. I guess I'd have to test drive one first. I haven't been in one since I was a kid. Maybe a Beetle would be better, then—or a Morris Minor, those are lovely too."

"You're really keen on that sort of thing, then? I wouldn't know what to do with an engine. I can just about manage to check the oil, but that's the limit of my expertise."

"Yeah. I love cars, and engines, anything like that," Nathan replied. "My dad does too. When I was a kid, I used to spend all weekend helping him do up whatever his latest project was. He got me hooked."

They'd both finished their drinks by now, and there were just a few crumbs left on the plate between them. Nathan licked his finger and pressed it down on the crumbs before transferring them to his mouth. He repeated the action, noticing

Owen was watching him. He deliberately licked his finger clean, enjoying the slightly glazed look on Owen's face. Nathan raised his eyebrows.

Owen grinned, caught out but unembarrassed. "Good thing you picked a cafe for our first date, or I'd already be trying to climb into your lap."

Nathan felt a prickle of heat sweep through him at the thought of it. He imagined the feel of Owen's legs wrapped around his waist and how Owen would look, smiling down at Nathan with his dark hair all messy from Nathan's hands and his lips wet from kissing.

Fuck.

Nathan definitely wasn't moving out from behind this table for a while. His face burned hot as he tried to will away his erection and cursed his vivid imagination.

"Do you want another drink? It's my round." Thankfully Owen seemed unaware of Nathan's predicament.

"Yes, please." Nathan would be glad for the chance to calm down while Owen went up to order. "Can I have a cup of tea this time?"

"Sure. Normal tea? Or Earl Grey or herbal or anything?"

"Normal, please."

"And shall I get more cake?"

"I can always manage more cake."

"Anything in particular?"

"No. I'm not fussy. Surprise me."

"Okay."

Nathan watched as Owen went to order. There was a bit of a queue, and Nathan enjoyed the opportunity to study him while he had his back to Nathan. His jeans were snug, showing off a nice-looking arse. Owen was a few inches shorter than Nathan — maybe about five ten to Nathan's six two — and slimmer too, all lean, toned muscle where Nathan was more bulky. But he was well proportioned with broad shoulders and slim hips.

As Owen reached the counter and turned, Nathan could see his profile. He watched as Owen spoke to the lady serving him, gesturing to the display of cakes. As she turned away to fetch something, Owen glanced round at Nathan and caught him staring. His face split in a grin, warm and easy but mischievous too. Owen had a slightly piratical look to him with his shaggy dark hair and stubbled jaw. Nathan's cheeks heated as he smiled back, embarrassed at being caught, but fuck it. They were on a date, after all. Owen knew Nathan was interested, even if he wanted to take things slowly. There was no shame in being caught ogling.

Owen returned to the table with a pot of tea for sharing, and a plate with two scones, jam, and clotted cream.

"Cool!" Nathan said. "I haven't had a cream tea in ages."

"Good. I'm glad you approve. I fancied a bit of nostalgia. My gran always gave us scones with clotted cream when I went round there for tea when I was a kid."

They got caught up in the ritual of pouring tea and splitting the scones in half, then piling on as much jam and cream as they could fit on them. Nathan's first half started falling apart as he was halfway through eating it, so he had to shove what was left in his mouth all in one go, trying to catch the crumbs with his spare hand. When he looked up, Owen was laughing at him. Nathan glared, his mouth too full to speak, and he had to fight back his own laughter otherwise he'd have choked.

"Classy." Owen was still chuckling.

But Nathan got his revenge when Owen had exactly the same trouble and even managed to drop clotted cream on his indigo jeans. He dabbed off as much of it as he could with a napkin, but it still showed.

"Bugger. It looks like someone's jizzed on me," he complained.

"Yeah, it kind of does."

Owen raised his head and stared at Nathan's mouth. "Well, I don't know why you're smirking, because you look like someone's jizzed on your face."

"What? Where?" Nathan wiped at his mouth.

"Yeah. You nearly got it. There's still a bit stuck in the corner, though." Owen raised his finger to point at his own lips. "No, the other side. Yep, that's it."

Nathan licked at the corner of his mouth, watching Owen's eyes follow the movement of his tongue. Owen looked hungry — and not for the other half of his scone that was still sitting on the plate. Nathan felt a thrill as he saw the heat in Owen's gaze, and he couldn't resist teasing him a little.

"Five more dates, and it could be the real thing." He held Owen's gaze and licked his lips again.

"Fucking hell," Owen hissed. "Are you trying to kill me?"

Nathan smiled innocently and picked up his tea.

When the plate was clean and they were down to their last dregs of tea, Owen asked the question that Nathan had been expecting to pop up at some point.

"So what happened with you while you were in London to make you come out? And why weren't you out before?"

43

Nathan stared into his nearly empty cup as though looking for answers there. "I wasn't completely sure before I left here, although I had a fair idea."

His cheeks heated. Nathan wasn't ready to admit that Owen had been a major catalyst in his realisation of his sexuality. He'd wondered before, but he hadn't been sure. Girls tended to throw themselves at him, and they'd been a distraction. He hadn't wanted to look too closely at the part of himself that looked at other guys in a way he knew wasn't appropriate for a straight guy. It had been easier to assume he was straight and run with that until he got to know Owen. Owen was so sure of himself he made being gay look easy. Nathan had envied him his certainty and confidence.

"When I lived in Bristol, I was still hooking up with girls. I hadn't done much with guys at all. But when I moved back to London it felt like a fresh start. Especially once I got a job and could move out of home."

"And you were ready to explore that side of yourself?" Owen asked, his tone serious.

"Yes."

"I get it. For me it was like that coming here. I just worked things out a little earlier than you, I guess."

Nathan nodded, meeting Owen's eyes again and seeing something softer there than he was used to. All Owen's usual teasing flirtiness was gone, and his attention was utterly focused on Nathan. It made something unfurl in Nathan's chest.

"Did you have a boyfriend in London?" Owen asked.

"Not really. I mean, there were a couple of guys I hooked up with more than once. But it never turned into anything serious."

"And you're not looking for one-offs anymore." It wasn't a question.

"No."

It wasn't that the one-night stands hadn't been fun sometimes. But Nathan had enjoyed the connection with the guys he'd spent more time with, and after a while, the one-night hookups had left him feeling he was missing out on something. But Nathan didn't want to articulate that to

Owen — the king of one-nighters. He didn't want come across as boring, or judgemental and disapproving, because he wasn't. But he knew what he wanted, and it was to find someone he could have something more meaningful than just sex with.

"Look," Nathan said, knotting his hands together on the table. "I don't want to put any pressure on you here. I didn't think you'd take me seriously when I suggested this dating thing, challenge, whatever you want to call it, and if you'd rather not bother, then I won't be offended."

Owen's brow furrowed, and Nathan searched his face, trying to work out what he was thinking. Then Owen slid his hand across the table and brushed his fingertips over Nathan's knuckles where they were clenched tight.

"I'm here, aren't I?" Owen said softly. His touch gave Nathan goosebumps. "Besides, next time I call my mam, I can tell her I'm dating a 'nice boy.'" Owen took his hand back to mime the air quotes. "It will make her year."

Nathan laughed. "I'm not always nice."

46

Owen gave him a filthy grin. "That's what I'm hoping."

When a waitress came to clear their table, they took it as their cue to leave. Nathan wouldn't have minded prolonging the date, but he couldn't have managed anything else to eat or drink, and maybe it was best to quit while they were ahead. It had been good, he thought. Owen had been fun to talk to, and there was definite attraction on both sides. Nathan was looking forward to exploring the chemistry between them.

They walked together a couple of hundred yards down Gloucester Road, then stopped by the crossing as their ways home parted there.

"Well, that was fun," Owen said.

"Yeah."

"You up for another date next weekend?"

Owen seemed uncertain, and Nathan was quick to smile and nod. "Yes, definitely."

"Any ideas about what you'd like to do? And is Saturday good for you again?"

"Not really." Nathan shrugged. "And yes, Saturday's fine."

"Okay. Keep it free, and I'll text you or call you, and we can work it out."

"Are you gonna make me wait till Thursday next week?" Nathan raised an eyebrow.

Owen chuckled. "Yeah, sorry. I was worried you were going to say no. Anyway, you can always call me instead."

They stood for a moment, looking at each other.

Nathan finally broke the awkward silence. "Okay. I'll see you next Saturday, then."

Owen nodded. "Thanks for today."

He stepped forwards and gave Nathan a quick one-armed hug and the barest brush of lips on his cheek. He pulled back before Nathan could do more than bring a hand up to touch Owen's shoulder. Nathan blinked, feeling his cheeks heat, and when he looked at Owen, Owen was pink-cheeked too.

The pedestrian crossing started to beep with the signal to cross.

"Bye then." Owen turned and hurried away before the cars started to move again.

"Goodbye," Nathan called after him. Then he turned and started walking home.

His phone buzzed in his pocket a few minutes later.

See. No waiting till Thurs this week ;)

Nathan grinned, and another text from Owen popped up before he could reply.

I wanna kiss you properly next time

Nathan's smile stretched even wider, and a bubble of happiness expanded in his chest.

Sounds good to me, he replied.

Chapter Three

When Owen got home, the smell of frying onions, garlic, and spices was wafting down the hallway. He followed the scent to the kitchen and found Jack stirring something in a saucepan. Simon was sitting at the kitchen table chopping peppers.

Simon looked up as Owen entered. "Hi. How did the date go?"

"I think it went pretty well." He tried to hold back a smile, but he couldn't stop his lips from curling as he thought about Nathan. He pulled out a chair and joined Simon at the table.

Simon narrowed his eyes. "You look very smug for someone who just sat around drinking coffee all afternoon. Did you blow him in the toilet?"

"Fuck off." Owen rolled his eyes. "In a cafe in the middle of the afternoon? Give me some credit.

Anyway, you know the score. I was hardly likely to wear him down on a first date, but I'm still hoping I might not have to wait for all five. I kissed him goodbye though."

"With tongue?"

"No. Just on the cheek."

"Aww." Simon fluttered his hand on his chest and pretended to swoon. "Look at my boy being all sweet and romantic. I never thought I'd see the day."

Owen nabbed a piece of pepper off the chopping board and threw it at him, sticking his tongue out.

"Seriously, though," Jack cut in. "It was good? You're seeing him again next weekend?"

"Yes, and yes."

Simon punched Owen lightly on the arm, not teasing this time. "That's great. Have you got any plans for what to do yet? Maybe you should try something more romantic next time. Impress him."

"I've got an idea I'm considering, but I haven't decided yet." Owen changed the subject. "So, what are you cooking, Jack? Is this a romantic dinner for two or are you making enough for me?"

"Chicken enchiladas, and I can make enough for three."

"Thanks. Need any help?"

"No, we've got it under control. But you can get me another beer."

"Oh yeah, me too, please." Simon drained the one in front of him. "If you're getting one for Jack."

Owen texted Nathan on Monday evening. He had a plan and wanted to make arrangements before Nathan suggested anything for the weekend.

Are you free on Saturday afternoon again? And maybe evening too?

Owen waited anxiously for Nathan's reply. It came about half an hour later.

Yes, and evening is ok too.

Owen did a mental fist pump. *Meet me in the Watershed cafe at 3?*

Ok, where are we going?

Wait and see, Owen replied.

They had no contact for the rest of the week, but on Saturday morning, Owen got a text from Nathan.

Prob a silly question, but does it matter what I wear?

Clothes :P

Nathan replied with, *well duh. I didn't think the Watershed had a clothing optional policy.*

Owen chuckled and texted back. *Crying shame. Srsly, wear whatever u like, we're not going anywhere fancy.*

Ok c u later.

Owen was relieved the weather was dry and bright, and warm for late April. His plans would have been less fun if it was pissing down with rain.

He got to the Watershed just before three. He couldn't see Nathan there yet, so he went up to the bar to order a coffee for himself. As the guy behind the bar was fiddling with the coffee machine, a hand touched Owen's shoulder.

"Hi, sorry — am I late?"

"No." Owen turned. "I was early. Hi."

They grinned at each other for a moment, and Owen enjoyed the rush of excitement that Nathan inspired in him. He wanted to kiss him, but wasn't sure how he would respond. If Owen had anything to do with it, there was definitely going to be kissing later today. No sex was one thing, but he needed contact. He wanted to find out if the sparks he felt in Nathan's presence would ignite the way he hoped when they touched one another. And if they did... then maybe Nathan could be persuaded to get dirty with Owen a little sooner than planned.

"Have you already ordered?" Nathan asked.

"Yeah, but I haven't paid yet, so I can get you something too. What do you want?"

When they'd got their order, they found a table and sat.

"So, are you going to tell me what we're doing this afternoon?" Nathan asked.

Owen felt a twinge of nerves, wondering if his idea would fall flat.

"We don't have to if you don't fancy it. But you said about liking engines and stuff… so I thought maybe we could go and see the *SS Great Britain* — unless you've been before?"

"No, I haven't. That would be awesome." Nathan's enthusiasm was clearly genuine. "I always wanted to when I was a student, but I never got around to it. Won't it be boring for you, though?"

"No. I've been before — my big sister dragged me there with her kids one weekend and it was actually pretty cool. I'd like to see it again."

"Great." Nathan's knee nudged Owen's under the table, and Nathan let it stay there.

Owen smiled and raised his coffee cup for a sip. "And are you okay to hang out later too? I thought we could go somewhere and eat after."

"Yes, sure."

The *SS Great Britain* was a big success. Even Owen had forgotten how interesting it was. When his sister made him go before, he'd expected it to be boring. But the way it was all set up hooked him, and he ended up reading all the stuff on display and really getting into it.

They took their time because Nathan wanted to see everything. Owen enjoyed watching him in the museum section they walked through first. He pored over the history of the ship and studied the old photographs of her. Owen had read it all before, so he spent more time looking at Nathan, enjoying his enthusiasm and feeling more than a little smug at the success of the venue he'd picked for their date.

As they stood looking at one of the displays, their arms brushed. Owen's heart rate picked up as he felt Nathan's fingers curl around his own and squeeze.

"This is cool." Nathan's voice was low and warm. "Thanks for bringing me here."

Owen squeezed back. "I'm glad it's a hit."

They released each other's hands as they moved on, but the warm feeling in Owen's chest persisted.

When they made it into the ship, Nathan headed straight for the engine room and stood, gazing in awe at the huge bits of machinery that had once powered the magnificent steamship in her heyday. It meant nothing to Owen, just lots of cogs and other things he didn't know the names of, but it was cool to see the daft grin on Nathan's face. Owen congratulated himself on being an awesome date chooser. If it hadn't been for their arrangement, he might have even hoped for a blowjob for being so thoughtful. But today he supposed he'd have to settle for a snog.

Owen's plans were vague for the evening, but he hoped that after dinner there would be ample opportunity for kissing if they walked back together in the dark.

He was surprised at his own eagerness for something as simple as a kiss. It was alien to him to have romantic feelings about someone. Maybe this taking-it-slow business wasn't so bad after all. Or maybe Nathan was getting under Owen's skin. Either way, Owen was buzzing with a strange and unfamiliar kind of energy. He felt unsettled but excited too.

It was busy on the boat when they first arrived, but as they progressed up through the decks it got quieter, maybe because it was nearly closing time.

Nathan had to stoop to get through the doorways when they went to look in the cabins.

"I wouldn't have fancied spending a long time on board this ship." He rubbed his head after misjudging one. "I'd have had a permanent egg on my head, or a cricked neck from stooping all the time."

"Better for short-arses like me," Owen agreed.

"You're not that short. And even you would have trouble sleeping on one of those." Nathan pointed to one of the bunks. He was right. There was no way an average-sized man would have been able to stretch out in one.

As they left that cabin, Nathan led the way into the next and then stopped abruptly with a gasp. Owen bumped into him. He put his hands on

Nathan's shoulders and peered over to see what had caused his reaction, then chuckled. "Creepy, aren't they?" He met the blank eyes of a waxwork model dressed in Victorian clothing. "They scared the crap out of me the first time I came here."

"It was the one in the bunk that made me jump," Nathan replied, sounding a little shaken. "It looks like a dead body. Bloody hell."

He turned, and Owen suddenly realised how close they were as his hands dropped away from Nathan's shoulders. The cabin was tiny, and Nathan was right there, all big, broad, and gorgeous, and looking at Owen with something in his eyes that Owen recognised — because he felt it too.

Owen made the first move, bringing a hand up to touch Nathan's cheek. But Nathan was the one who dipped his head to close the gap and press their lips together. The kiss was soft and mostly chaste. But the touch of Nathan's lips sent a jolt of want through Owen that was so strong, his knees felt momentarily wobbly. He parted his lips to taste Nathan and slid his hand around to the back of

Nathan's neck, holding him close. But then the sound of running footsteps and children's voices approaching made them break apart, grinning and flushed.

"More of that later?" Owen suggested.

Nathan nodded. "Yeah."

He looked a little dazed. Owen was glad it wasn't just him who felt that way.

"Come on, let's go up on deck. Otherwise we won't have time to see it all before they close."

Owen led the way, with Nathan on his heels as they passed a gaggle of kids and a dad with a baby in a carrier. The kids shrieked and giggled when they found the figures in the cabin.

Up on the deck of the ship, it was still sunny but cooler now the sun was low in the sky. The breeze had picked up while they'd been indoors, and Owen wished he'd brought a hat or an extra layer. They stood and looked out over the railings at the harbour, where a couple of swans drifted by like stately ships. A gust of wind made Owen pop up the collar of his jacket as he tried to suppress a shiver.

"Are you cold?" Nathan moved closer so their shoulders were pressed together.

"Yeah," Owen admitted. "I always get caught out at this time of year. The sun comes out, and I forget it can still be chilly in the evenings. It's my eternal optimism."

Nathan chuckled. "Optimism is good. But I think we're done here. Are you ready to move on?"

"Okay. Are you hungry yet? Or do you want to go somewhere for a drink before we eat?"

"Maybe a beer first, but I'm easy."

Owen snorted. "No, you're not. Mr Five Dates Before We Fuck."

He was only teasing, but when he glanced sideways, Nathan's face had pulled into a frown.

"Yeah, I know it was a stupid idea," he said. "I feel like an idiot about it already."

A spike of unexpected guilt shot through Owen. He turned and put out a hand to cover Nathan's where he was gripping the railing.

"Hey," he said lightly, waiting till Nathan turned to meet his eyes. "Okay, so maybe at first it

61

seemed like a stupid idea. But you know? After one-and-a-half dates, it's not looking so bad."

Nathan looked uncertain. "Really?"

"Yeah." Owen squeezed Nathan's hand. "I mean... I'm not saying it will be easy. But this dating thing is kind of fun."

And Owen meant it, even if he was still going to try and persuade Nathan to hurry things along a little—because he was crap at being patient.

"Good."

It was quiet up on deck now with just ten minutes till closing time, and nobody seemed to be paying any attention to them. So Owen stretched up and pressed a kiss to Nathan's cheek, catching one of his dimples as he smiled.

After they left the SS Great Britain, they stopped at a pub for a quick drink, but the smell of the food being served there made both of them realise they were hungry.

"Do you want to eat here?" Owen asked. "The food looks pretty good, but I'd been thinking we could go to Za Za Bazaar. Have you been there before?"

"No, but I've heard of it. Is it the eat-all-you-can buffet place back near the Watershed?"

"Yeah, it's really cool. It's set up like a food market, and it's massive inside. There's literally every sort of food you can think of — Indian, Chinese, sushi, pizza, burgers... it's amazing."

"That sounds like fun." Nathan patted his belly. "You're making me hungry just thinking about it. Drink up, then, and we can head over."

They had no trouble getting a table as it was still relatively early, and they ordered more beer to drink. They gravitated towards the Asian food — in Owen's opinion it was the best stuff there, although all of it was pretty good.

As they ate, they talked about their families. They hadn't known each other well enough at uni to know those kinds of personal details, so they filled each other in on their parents and siblings and what their upbringing had been like.

"Four sisters?" Nathan chuckled. "So you and your dad were swamped by a sea of oestrogen."

"Yeah." Owen grinned. "Then after my parents split up, it was just me. But it wasn't so bad."

Owen was close to his mam and his sisters — two older and two younger — but he'd never had a good relationship with his dad. It had almost been a relief when he'd moved out when Owen was thirteen. They'd clashed over everything, and Owen had felt like he was a constant source of disappointment. He wasn't sporty enough… wasn't masculine enough… was interested in video games when he should have been interested in girls…. He was interested in boys too, of course, but he kept that quiet till he was eighteen. When he came out, shortly before he left home to go to uni, it was no big surprise to his dad, but it hammered another nail into the coffin of their relationship. Owen didn't see much of him these days, and that suited him fine.

"Do you go back home to visit often?" Nathan asked. "It's not very far for you."

Owen was from Abergavenny in South Wales, only about an hour from Bristol.

"Yeah, I try and get back there every few weeks. Mam likes to have a gathering on a Sunday sometimes, cook a big roast, and get me and my big sisters home for it."

"Yeah. My mum likes it when she manages to get all the family back," Nathan said. "It only usually happens at Christmas these days, though, with Ben — my older brother — up in Glasgow now.

"Is it just the two of you?"

"Yes." Nathan nodded. "Ben's twenty-seven — five years older than me."

"Do you get on?"

"Mostly. We fought when he still lived at home — the usual sibling bickering, you know how it is."

Owen chuckled his agreement. He might be close to his sisters now, but they'd had their moments while they were growing up.

"We get on pretty well these days, but with him being up in Scotland, I don't see much of him."

"How did your family take you coming out?"

"They were great. I wasn't too worried about telling them. I knew they'd be okay. I just wanted to be sure I was ready before I did it. You can't take it back once it's out there, can you?"

"True."

Nathan picked up his beer bottle and drank. Owen admired the bob of his throat as he swallowed. Nathan caught him looking as he put his drink back down and smiled, dimples denting his cheeks. Owen wanted to kiss him again, but he settled for smiling back and nudging Nathan's knee with his own under the table.

"Have you got room for more food?" Owen asked. Their plates were empty now.

"Seems a shame not to try a few more things. I want to try the pizza, and maybe get a couple more of those spring rolls."

After they'd eaten, they decided to walk home rather than get a bus, and it wasn't far for either of them. They were both full after being unable to resist a third trip around the food stalls, and a bit of exercise and fresh air seemed like a good idea.

After they'd passed the Hippodrome theatre, Nathan hesitated at the next junction.

"I'd normally walk this way home, but is it quicker for you if we go straight on here?"

"I'll walk your way," Owen replied. "It's not much of a detour."

Plus the streets were quieter and darker this way, and Owen had plans that required a little more privacy than they'd get if they walked up the main drag past all the pubs and fast-food joints.

He took Nathan's hand as they walked, reassured when he laced their fingers together. They made their way up the dark streets away from the centre and through the quieter residential streets. Nathan hesitated again as they reached a junction where it would have made sense for Owen to turn off if he was going back to his place.

"Do you need to go that way now?"

"No, it's okay. I'll walk this way a little more. It's a nice night anyway, and I'm not in a hurry."

It was a lovely evening — a little chilly, but the wind had dropped again, and Owen was warm from the effort of walking up the hills from the city centre. With Nathan's hand wrapped warmly around his, Owen wasn't in a hurry to part ways.

"I'm not a girl. You don't need to walk me home." Nathan's voice was light, and he squeezed Owen's fingers as they set off again.

"Believe me. I'm well aware you're not a girl." Owen bumped Nathan with his shoulder. "I don't date girls."

"You don't usually date guys either."

"No. But most guys aren't as high maintenance as you," Owen teased. "Here, let's walk through the park."

He tugged on Nathan's hand, steering him away from the road and down a path that led to a grassy, tree-lined space with a children's play area at the bottom of a dip.

"Oh, I see where this is going."

Nathan glanced sideways at Owen. The dim orange light from the street lamps was just enough for Owen to see his expression of amusement.

"I have no idea what you're talking about." Owen tried — and failed — to sound innocent. "I like parks at night. They're peaceful."

"And secluded."

"And swings are cool, and people glare at you if you use them in the daytime when you're twenty-three years old and don't have any kids with you."

Nathan laughed. "Ah, we're here for the swings. Of course. But won't they be too small for us?"

"Nope. They've got ones here that are meant for big kids — like me."

Owen wasn't lying when he said he liked swings. So that was where they went, finally breaking their grip on each other's hands so they could take a swing each.

"I haven't been on a swing in years," Nathan said a little breathlessly once they'd got a rhythm going and were swooping in a high arc. "It's awesome."

Owen whooped as his swing reached its highest point and then dropped again, leaving him with a lurch of excitement and adrenaline. "Yeah," he agreed. "Told you. Swings are cool."

They got competitive, each trying to outdo the other until they tired of it and let them slow down gradually until they were rocking gently, their feet back on the ground.

"So you really did just bring me here to swing," Nathan said. "I feel bad for suspecting ulterior motives now."

Owen smiled to himself, not sure whether Nathan could make out his expression in the almost darkness. "Well, there *are* other things we could do."

There was a short pause.

"Oh yes?" Nathan sounded hopeful.

Taking that as permission, Owen left his swing and moved to stand in front of Nathan's, just as Nathan's swing drifted gently forwards. Their knees bumped, and Owen caught the chains of the swing, holding it there.

"Hey." He grinned down at Nathan, who returned the smile.

Owen let go of the chains and let Nathan swing backwards, but when he swung back, Owen caught him again.

"Tease," Nathan huffed.

"Not this time."

Owen leaned down and kissed him, gently at first. But when he tried to draw back, Nathan made a muffled noise of protest and brought a hand up to tangle in Owen's hair, keeping him there and deepening the kiss. Owen smiled against Nathan's mouth and opened up, letting Nathan's tongue touch his own. But the angle was awkward with Owen needing to bend to reach Nathan properly. He disentangled himself for a moment.

"Hang on, this isn't very comfortable, let me…."

He pushed Nathan back again, so Nathan was standing more than sitting now. His feet were on the ground, but the seat of the swing stopped him from falling backwards as Owen pressed up against him, fitting his hips between Nathan's parted thighs and resuming the kiss with even more intensity.

Nathan hummed into Owen's mouth and put his hands on his hips, pulling him closer, and Owen's dick tingled with a rush of blood as their

71

groins came into contact. He was getting hard fast and suspected Nathan was too. He couldn't resist finding out, so he pushed a little against Nathan until he felt an answering hardness against his.

Hungry for more, Owen broke away from Nathan's lips and kissed his way down his neck. He breathed in the heady mix of man, and skin, and a hint of shower gel, and stopped to enjoy it for a moment, licking and kissing gently so that he wouldn't leave marks where they'd show.

Nathan's breathing was ragged. One of his hands was in Owen's hair again, massaging Owen's scalp with his fingertips and sending delicious sensations down Owen's spine that stoked his arousal higher.

"Fuck, that's good," Nathan murmured, and his throat vibrated under Owen's tongue.

Owen drew back and grinned. "Yeah."

But he didn't want to waste time talking when they could be kissing, so he cupped Nathan's face in both hands and smashed their lips together again, messier this time with a dirty grind of his hips.

It was quiet in the park. The noise of the city was a low hum that barely intruded on the wet sounds of their kisses and the rasp of their breathing. They were snogging like teenagers, all urgency and desperation but not leading anywhere. God, how Owen wished it was. His cock was aching to be stroked or sucked, and from the way Nathan was clutching greedily at Owen, he seemed pretty horny too.

Nathan had both hands on Owen's arse now, squeezing and pulling him closer. Owen suddenly realised he was close to coming and was almost at the point of not even caring and walking home with wet underwear. But the roar of a car, gunning fast along the quiet road beside the park, made them startle and break the kiss.

They were breathing hard, and Nathan's face was slack and glazed in the dim light, his mouth shiny with spit. Owen imagined Nathan dropping to his knees and letting Owen push his cock slowly between those lips.

When the car had passed, Nathan reached for Owen again.

73

But Owen stopped him with a firm hand on his chest.

"Unless you want me to break our no-jizz rule, we need to stop. Because I'm about thirty seconds away from coming in my pants if we carry on like this."

Nathan sighed. "Yeah, good point. Me too."

They stared at each other for a moment.

"I guess it's time to head home, then?" Nathan said.

Owen slid his hand from Nathan's chest to the bulge in his trousers and cupped it.

"Are you sure you don't want to invite me in— for coffee?" He rubbed the hard line of Nathan's erection with the heel of his hand. God, he felt good. Owen wanted to see it, to touch his skin, to taste him.

But Nathan gripped Owen's wrist and pulled his hand away. "We had a deal, remember?"

"Deals are made to be broken." Owen tried to reach down again, but Nathan squeezed Owen's wrist hard, keeping his hand away from its goal.

"That's not even an expression." Nathan's voice was firm. "And I meant it when I said I don't just want to be a casual fuck. I know it might seem stupid or prudish to you, but I'm not taking you home tonight."

Owen felt his cheeks flush hot in the cool air, and his ardour was doused abruptly as guilt washed over him.

"I'm sorry," he said roughly. "I just...." But all his excuses sounded pathetic. "Sorry," he said again.

"It's okay." Nathan released his wrist and eased off the swing to stand. "It's no big deal."

Owen walked with Nathan to the end of the road where they'd finally need to go their separate ways. The mood between them had soured a little, and Owen was angry with himself for spoiling what had been a really great evening until he pushed Nathan too far. But they agreed to keep next Saturday free for another date.

"Are you sure you want to?" Nathan asked.

Owen couldn't read his face, his expression didn't give much away, but his jaw was tight.

75

Owen's stomach lurched as he wondered if Nathan was having second thoughts about this whole thing. "I do if you do."

Owen wasn't a quitter, and damn it, he wanted Nathan. He could be patient if he had to. And after they'd had their five dates? Well... who knew how he'd be feeling then. But there was no point worrying about that until it came to it.

"Okay. Next Saturday, then."

They gave each other a quick hug, but there was no more kissing.

Owen missed it already.

Chapter Four

Nathan was feeling flat when he got home. He went straight to his room, avoiding the living room where he could hear the sound of the TV. He wasn't in the mood for a date post-mortem with Kirsty right now, and he knew she'd quiz him for details. He was horny and irritable — annoyed with Owen for being pushy, but also with himself for turning Owen down, and that didn't make any sense. He couldn't have it both ways.

He stripped down to his boxers and T-shirt and got into bed. His palmed his cock as it stiffened under his touch, thinking about Owen grinding against him in the park. It would have been so easy for them to have carried on until they came, or stroked each other off there in the darkness. And God... it would have been hot. Nathan slipped his hand under the waistband of his boxers and sighed as he wrapped his fingers around his cock so he could stroke himself properly.

He was just getting into a nice rhythm, which would be guaranteed to get him off fast, when his phone buzzed on the nightstand.

"Bollocks," he muttered, torn between ignoring it and looking to see who the message was from. But the distraction had pulled him out of his fantasy anyway, so he reached across with his free hand to grab his phone.

Thx for a fun night, sorry I spoilt it at the end

Owen. A smile crept over Nathan's face.

He took his hand off his cock and wiped the precome on his boxers so he could type a reply.

It's okay, u didn't. It was good.

He waited to see if Owen would reply again. He didn't have to wait long.

Really?

Nathan huffed in amusement. It wasn't like Owen to sound so unsure of himself.

Really. He paused, then typed. *Maybe a little too good.*

The reply was almost instant.

???

Nathan grinned, considering for a moment. Then he gave in to the urge for mischief. Owen wanted dirty? He could have dirty. But it was going to be on Nathan's terms.

Yeah. U got me all riled up. He pressed send, then immediately added. *I was dealing but then u interrupted…*

Fuck came the reply. Then, *Don't let me stop u. In fact I might join in.*

Nathan's cock jerked as if in protest at not being touched, and when he looked down, there was a wet patch seeping through the fabric of his boxers.

Sounds like a plan, he managed. And then he put his phone down beside him, stripped his T-shirt off and turned his attention back to his neglected dick.

It was an embarrassingly short amount of time before Nathan shot all over his stomach and chest to mental images of Owen doing exactly the same thing. As he was wiping himself clean with his discarded T-shirt and getting his breath back, his phone buzzed again.

Well that didn't take long

Nathan chuckled. *Same,* he replied.

Owen's next reply took a little longer.

Does this violate no orgasms rule? Is the challenge now officially fucked? (pun intended)

No, this doesn't count. Nathan typed back. *Orgasms ok as long as we're not together.*

So where do u stand on phone sex? Owen shot back.

Nathan blinked at his screen. Phone sex sounded interesting. He'd never tried that, and it might be fun.

I'm open to persuasion ;) night Owen
Night x

The subject of phone sex didn't come up again that week. But they did text each other quite a bit — sometimes rather suggestively. But on Wednesday evening, Owen phoned Nathan while he was doing some press-ups in the living room after he'd been out for a cycle.

Nathan was out of breath when he answered. "Hey."

"Hi. Did I interrupt something?" Owen asked, and Nathan was suddenly very aware of how loudly he was breathing.

Nathan laughed. "Only press-ups. Sorry to disappoint."

"Damn. Well… I can use my imagination instead, then, because you sound much the same as you might if I'd caught you doing something more interesting."

"So what did you want, Owen?" Nathan's muscles were stiff and tired, and he was in dire need of a hot shower, so he wasn't in the mood for talking.

"I was thinking about Saturday. You're all outdoorsy and stuff, aren't you? How do you fancy a walk up a hill in Wales, and then dinner in a country pub somewhere before we drive back?"

"Oh yeah, that sounds great," Nathan replied. "One of the downsides of having no car is that I don't get out of the city much."

"Okay." Owen sounded pleased with himself. "I'll pick you up after lunch on Saturday then, at about two o'clock, if that's okay?"

"Sure."

"I'm in the supermarket, and I'm nearly at the front of the queue now, so I'll let you get back to your press-ups — if that's what you were really doing."

"I'm in the living room, and Kirsty's home. I'm definitely not doing anything other than press-ups." Nathan lowered his voice a little. "But maybe I will in the shower in a few minutes."

"Nice," Owen replied. "I'm totally imagining that scenario now, just so you know. And that's not at all helpful in a public place."

"Sorry."

"You don't sound sorry at all."

"Funny, that. Bye, Owen."

Nathan ended the call, chuckling at the thought of a flustered Owen at the supermarket checkout.

Nathan was ready and waiting when Owen rang his doorbell on Saturday afternoon. When he opened the door, Owen looked him up and down and grinned.

"I'm digging the Boy Scout look."

Nathan quirked an eyebrow. "At least I'm appropriately dressed for hillwalking." He looked pointedly at Owen's skinny jeans and fashionable, rather than practical, trainers.

"These will do fine." Owen shrugged. "It's not like we're going anywhere too adventurous. Nice legs, by the way."

Nathan was wearing cargo shorts, which showed off his knees and calves above his thick socks and walking boots. He had fair skin, and it was sunny outside, so he'd plastered some suntan lotion on them, which had flattened down his usual blond fuzz of leg hair.

He couldn't decide whether Owen was taking the piss or not, so he ignored the comment and followed Owen out to his car.

"What's in the bag?" Owen asked as he opened the boot for Nathan to stow the small rucksack he was carrying.

"A couple of water bottles, suntan lotion, a waterproof jacket—just in case—and a few snacks."

"Snacks? Awesome. Are there some for me?"

"Hmm." Nathan pretended to consider it. "I suppose I can share."

He got into the passenger seat, his feet rustling on discarded crisp packets and chocolate wrappers.

"Sorry it's such a state in here." Owen started the engine. "I'm in the car so much of my day with all the travelling for my job. It always ends up full of crap."

"Where are we going then?" Nathan asked as Owen put the car in gear and pulled out. "Is it far?"

"About an hour," Owen replied. "There's a nice walk up one of the hills near my hometown. And there's a good pub near there too—for food after."

"Sounds fun. Do you need me to map read or anything?"

"Nah. I know it like the back of my hand. It's almost like driving home for me." Owen glanced sideways and flashed Nathan a grin. His Welsh accent was more pronounced today, Nathan noticed. Just the prospect of driving over the bridge into his home country seemed to have brought it out. It was sexy.

Owen handled the car confidently through the city traffic, driving north out of Bristol until they got to the motorway. Then he put his foot down and let the powerful engine eat up the miles until they reached the huge bridge that led over the river into Wales.

The roads got smaller and windier as they snaked their way through the valleys and Owen had to slow right down. He pointed out local landmarks as he drove, and Nathan admired the countryside. It was wonderful to be out of the city.

"I wish I'd grown up somewhere like this. It was all housing estates and suburbia where I lived."

"But you could get the train into London anytime you wanted," Owen said. "I'd have killed to have been closer to a city."

"You're not that far from Cardiff, surely?"

"Yeah. But there isn't a station near where I lived, and the bus service was crap. I didn't get there very often." Owen was quiet for a moment as he navigated a particularly sharp bend. "It is gorgeous here, though." His voice had softened. "I appreciate it more now I don't live here, but that's always the way of it, I suppose. I like Bristol too, and it's not too far for me to visit."

"Would you ever move back here?" Nathan asked.

Owen shrugged. "I don't know. Maybe when I'm older and tired of the city, but at the moment it suits me better. I could live here and commute for work if I wanted, but all my mates are in Bristol. I haven't kept in touch with many people from back home."

A few miles farther along, Owen pointed. "See that hill over there? That's where we're headed."

Nathan looked at the hill where it rose out of the surrounding farmland, steep sided and wooded on the slopes. It was ridge shaped, with a sloping spine like a giant, sleeping animal.

"It's beautiful. Looks like a good walk."

"Perfect day for it too," Owen replied. "I don't think you'll be needing that waterproof."

It certainly looked as if the weather was set fair.

"I might leave it in the car, save me carrying more than I need."

The car park at the start of the trail was busy, but they managed to find a space. Nathan repacked his bag, leaving the unwanted raincoat behind, and hitched it onto his back.

"Let's go then."

The first section of path was flat, leading to the edge of the woods. But as soon as they reached the trees, the trail began to climb steeply. The woods were beautiful — huge beeches and ancient oaks that made a canopy, blocking the sun and giving a

87

dappled, green shade. They passed several other people who were on their way back down, walkers in pairs or groups, some alone, some with kids and dogs.

Nathan let Owen set the pace. Nathan ran and cycled regularly, and he wasn't sure how fit Owen was — although he looked in pretty good shape. But Owen walked at a good speed, and they overtook a few older walkers and family groups with smaller children as the trail zigzagged up the steep hillside.

They stopped in a clearing for a rest and a drink. There was a large fallen tree, and they leaned against the trunk in the sunshine.

"Aren't you glad I brought water now?" Nathan passed the bottle to Owen.

"Yeah, I'm really thirsty. Glad one of us is good at planning ahead."

Nathan looked back down the path they'd climbed. "It's a shame we can't see the view. We must be quite high up by now."

"Once we get out of the trees we will, it won't be long now."

Just as they reached the edge of the woods there was a narrow section of path and they had to go in single file. Nathan went ahead, climbing up the uneven rocky slope with Owen following behind.

"The view from here is pretty great." Owen's voice made Nathan pause and frown for a moment, confused as he looked around at the trees. Sure, they were beautiful. But it wasn't very different to what they'd seen for the last half hour as they'd made their way up through the woodland. "Seriously. It's stunning." The amusement in Owen's voice finally clued Nathan in, and he turned his head to see Owen's gaze fixed on his arse.

"Oh yeah?" Nathan grinned, wiggling deliberately as he started moving again, but he kept his tone innocent. "Yes, the trees are beautiful, aren't they."

"Gorgeous," Owen agreed.

As they finally emerged from the trees onto the exposed grassy crest of the hill, Owen put a hand on Nathan's hip to stop him. "Look," he said.

Nathan turned and gazed out over the countryside spread out below them. "Wow."

"Yeah." Owen moved to stand beside him, their arms brushing as they stopped to drink it in. "I love how tiny the cars look from up here." He pointed, and Nathan followed his finger to watch a car making its way along the road down in the valley. It looked like a shiny beetle, crawling along on the green patchwork quilt of farmland.

They turned back to where the path stretched ahead of them. Wide and well trodden, it led up the spine of the hill over short, cropped grass interspersed with rocky crags. It was less steep now. The hard work of the climb was behind them, but there was still quite a way to go.

It took them another half hour or so to reach the trig point at the far end of the hill. There were several other walkers up there. Nathan and Owen waited for some kids to finish balancing on the stone marker that showed the highest point of the hill, then they leaned against it and looked out at the view again.

"This is great." Nathan stared at the view. "I've missed doing stuff like this."

Owen got his phone out of his pocket. "Hilltop selfie?" he suggested. He put his arm around Nathan and leaned in close to take the picture, getting in both their faces and the rocks and sky behind them. A gust of wind caught them as he took the picture, and a strand of Owen's hair blew into Nathan's face. He batted it away, chuckling.

"You've got too much hair."

"You're just jealous of my luscious locks. Hang on, I'll try again."

Owen tucked the errant strand behind his ear, and the second photo worked better. Their smiles were even wider that time.

"Now. Did somebody say something about snacks?" Owen asked. "What have you got in your bag?"

They climbed a little way down the rocky hilltop to find a spot that was both secluded and sheltered from the wind. They sat, leaning against the sun-warmed stone, and Nathan delved into his bag and pulled out some slightly squashed hot cross buns and a Thermos.

"It's hot chocolate. I always think tea and coffee taste weird out of a flask."

They passed the one cup between them, sharing the hot chocolate and eating the buns. Their fingers touched every time the cup changed hands, and Nathan felt a warmth in his belly that wasn't just from the hot drink.

When they'd finished, they sat a little longer with the sun on their faces. Nathan closed his eyes and tilted his head back, listening to the sound of a skylark high above and the occasional baa of a sheep in the distance.

"Thank you," Nathan said, his eyes still shut. "This is a perfect date."

He felt the weight of Owen's hand on his thigh, and when Nathan opened his eyes and turned his head, Owen was smiling at him.

"Yeah, it's pretty good."

Nathan leaned closer and kissed him. It was a sweet kiss, slow and lingering, and Nathan covered

Owen's hand with his own, slotting their fingers together and squeezing with warm pressure.

When they drew apart, they were both grinning like fools. Nathan wondered what was going on in Owen's head. He seemed to be taking to dating like a duck to water, but Nathan was still unsure of his motives. He didn't want to spoil things by asking, though, so he kept quiet.

After sitting in the sun for a while, they scrambled around on the rocks, challenging each other to find different ways up to the top of a small outcrop. Nathan was impressed with the way Owen moved on the rock. He was a natural climber, fearless and agile.

"Have you done much climbing?" Nathan asked as he watched Owen heave his body up and over onto a flat shelf of rock. "You look like you know what you're doing."

"Not on rocks," Owen replied. "I used to climb up a lot of trees as a kid, though, and out of my bedroom window when I was a teenager, until my mam caught me and grounded me for a week."

Nathan laughed. "What about indoor climbing? There's a couple of good indoor walls in Bristol."

"No, never tried it." Owen held a hand out to Nathan and helped him up onto the ledge beside him. "Maybe I should."

On the way back down the hill, they walked close together, smiling whenever they caught each other's eye. When they reached the wooded section, Owen took Nathan's hand and led him off the path.

"Where are we going?" Nathan asked.

"Somewhere we can do more kissing—kissing is allowed, right?"

Nathan's heart flip-flopped with excitement. "Yeah." He licked his lips. "Kissing is definitely allowed."

Once they were safely away from the path, Owen stopped by a huge oak tree, keeping the tree between them and the trail. "This'll do nicely."

He looked at Nathan with such heat in his eyes, that Nathan was half-hard with anticipation even before Owen grabbed his belt loops and reeled him in, kissing him deep and dirty until Nathan broke away to catch his breath.

"Fuck," he muttered against the warm damp skin of Owen's neck.

Owen snorted. "On our third date? What kind of tart do you take me for?"

Nathan drew back to see his teasing expression. "I know exactly what kind of tart you are."

"But you like me anyway." There was challenge in Owen's dark brown eyes now.

"Yeah," Nathan admitted. "I do."

And he did, more than he'd ever expected. But Nathan didn't want to think about that right now. He wanted to lose himself in Owen for a while.

He leaned down and claimed Owen's lips again, pressing him back into the tree trunk with the weight of his body as he kissed him, even more hungrily now. They kissed, messy and urgent, moving their hips against each other. Nathan's cock was trapped and catching uncomfortably against the zip of his shorts, so he pulled away and reached into his underwear, adjusting himself to a better angle. Owen watched the movement of Nathan's hand and when he met Nathan's gaze again, his eyes were dark and desperate-looking.

"I want to touch you so badly," he muttered. "Or blow you. God, I want to make you come."

Heat flooded the pit of Nathan's stomach, and his cock throbbed at the thought of it. It would be so easy to give in to temptation. But he took a ragged breath and managed to shake his head.

Owen's eyebrows drew down in a frown, but then he grinned wickedly. "Have you got a mobile signal?"

"What?" Nathan had no idea where that question had come from.

"Phone sex." Owen got his phone out of his pocket. "I could go and stand behind the next tree along. You said phone sex was allowed." But then his face fell. "Oh bugger. No signal at all."

Nathan wasn't sure whether he was relieved or disappointed. Maybe a bit of both. "Probably for the best," he said in the end.

It would have been a bit risky trying it in… well, not exactly a public place, but it wasn't ideal. Other walkers might stray from the main path looking for a quiet spot for a piss or something.

"Later, then?" Owen asked.

"Maybe." Nathan couldn't stop the smile that tugged at the corners of his lips.

Owen took Nathan's face in his hands and kissed him again. Slowly now, winding down into something gentle — if not quite chaste.

Nathan held him close. *Damn*, Owen felt good in Nathan's arms. Like he was meant to be there.

Owen took Nathan for dinner at a beautiful old pub in the middle of nowhere. They sat at a table for two, tucked away in a corner, and flirted shamelessly with each other as they ate. They took every opportunity to brush fingers, and they let their feet and legs tangle together under the small table, touching each other with subtle pressure and the promise of something unspoken. Nathan was in a glorious haze of infatuation, basking in Owen's attention.

On the drive back, they arranged to keep next Saturday free again for date number four.

"I want to take you somewhere next week," Nathan said. "You picked the last two places. So it's definitely my turn."

"Okay. Where's it gonna be?"

"It's a surprise," Nathan replied. "You'll have to wait and see."

"Sounds fun. I like surprises."

When they got back to Nathan's flat, Owen found a parking space and turned off the engine. It was early evening now, but still light.

Nathan turned to Owen. "Thanks for a really great date. The walk was beautiful. I loved it."

"I'm so glad. I wasn't sure if it was a bit… I don't know. A weird thing to do on a date."

"It was perfect," Nathan insisted.

They held each other's gaze for a moment.

"So… I'll see you next week, then."

They both moved at the same time, leaning awkwardly across the handbrake to meet in a clumsy kiss. Nathan brought his hand up to Owen's head, sliding his fingers into Owen's hair where it was tangled from the wind on the hilltop. Their stubble scratched, but Owen's lips were soft and warm.

They were both grinning when they parted.

"Yeah. See you next week," Owen replied. "I might call you later, though." His smile turned suggestive, and Nathan flushed hot at the implication. But he wasn't complaining.

"Okay."

Talking to Owen later sounded like it might be fun. Nathan thought he'd be up for trying whatever Owen had in mind.

Kirsty was curled up on the sofa when Nathan let himself in. She greeted him, pausing the TV to ask, "How was your date?"

Nathan couldn't hold back a goofy smile as he replied. "It was awesome. We went to Wales."

"Wales?" Kirsty raised her eyebrows. "What... did he take you to meet his mum or something? Christ, it *must* be serious."

"God, no. He took me hillwalking. It was great—really beautiful."

"It sounds surprisingly innocent. When you told me the deal with the five dates, I was expecting more along the lines of seedy night clubs and gay saunas than local history and country walks. Maybe he's lulling you into a false sense of security before he steps up his game?"

Kirsty grinned, obviously teasing, but Nathan felt a surge of irritation and protectiveness.

"You make him sound like some creepy sexual predator. And it's not like that. Yeah... okay, there *is* a bit of a competition going on, I guess, where he's trying to wear me down and I'm trying to hold off for a little longer. But it's all good-natured, and Owen's not nearly as bad as you're making out." Nathan put his backpack down and sat on the sofa by Kirsty's feet before continuing. "I suppose Owen's surprised me too. He's been so thoughtful in picking the venues for the last two dates. He chose them because he guessed I'd enjoy them."

"That's sweet." Kirsty was serious now. "I wish I could find a bloke who put so much thought into dating. All the dates I've been on have involved beer, and — if I'm lucky — dinner and a film They're not exactly imaginative. Do you know where he's taking you next weekend?"

"It's my turn to choose next." Nathan smiled. "And I've already decided."

"Ooh, where are you taking him?"

"I'm going to take him climbing. He's never been, but he's a natural. We did a bit of bouldering up on the rocks today, and I think he'll love it."

"Outdoors? Do you have the gear for it?"

"I thought I'd take him indoors for his first time. Anyway, I don't have transport. If I made him drive, it would spoil the surprise. We can walk to the indoor wall from here. Then we can go for drinks or dinner after."

"That sounds like a great date too. Seriously, I need to find a man with imagination. Maybe you and Owen are well suited after all."

Nathan's cheeks heated as he admitted, "Yeah. Maybe we are. I hope so anyway. I was expecting this just to be a bit of a laugh, but underneath all his bravado, he's...." He hesitated for a moment. "I don't know... sweet, I guess, and a good person."

Kirsty looked at him intently, a small frown on her face.

"What?" Nathan asked.

"You're really into him, aren't you?"

Nathan shrugged, about to deflect, but Kirsty continued.

"I don't get why you're still holding out. You like him and he seems to be making the effort with the dating thing. So why are you still waiting to have sex with him?"

Nathan shrugged. It was a hard question to answer because, honestly, he wasn't quite sure why it mattered to him. "I'm stubborn, I guess? We made a deal, and I want to see if he'll see it through. I want him. But I'm not sure I trust him. For all I know, he still just sees me as a conquest. At least if I make him wait the full five dates, then whatever happens after that — it's on my terms, not his."

"Control freak." Kirsty chuckled.

"Maybe." Nathan grinned back. "I quite like the power."

"Poor Owen," she said. "I almost feel sorry for him now."

Later, in bed, Nathan lay awake and thought about Owen. Kirsty's words kept replaying in his head. *You're really into him.* Nathan couldn't hide from it. He'd known from the start this was a dangerous game. Owen had the potential to hurt him if this didn't work out, because Nathan cared too much about him already, and it was only date three. But what was Nathan going to do — call it off? No way was that happening. Not when things were going so well. He just had to hope that Owen might be developing feelings for him too.

Because Nathan was falling, and it was too late to stop.

Chapter Five

Owen sat in the living room, staring at his phone. He was desperate to text or call Nathan like he'd promised, but he was trying to hold out till a little later. Just before bed might be a good time for what Owen had in mind.

"You know what they say about watched pots."

"Huh, what?" Owen looked up to meet Simon's amused gaze from where he was curled up next to Jack on the sofa.

"They never boil." Jack finished the adage, glancing meaningfully at the phone in Owen's hand.

"Oh, sod off. I'm not even waiting for anything anyway. I told him I'd call." Owen put his phone on the coffee table and leaned back in his chair.

Simon was still grinning at him.

"What's so funny?" Owen glared back.

"You're really hooked. I've never seen you like this over a guy before."

Owen opened his mouth. His first instinct was to deny everything. But as he felt a hot tingling flush flood his cheeks, he realised he probably wasn't going to convince anyone.

"Well, you're hardly one to talk." He glared at Simon, leaning into Jack's side like a conjoined twin, their hands entwined on Jack's thigh.

Simon smiled and squeezed Jack's hand. "I wasn't saying it's a bad thing. In fact, I recommend it. So anyway, what's going to happen at the end of these five dates — apart from all the sex, of course — have you thought about that?"

Owen shrugged. "I don't know. I suppose we'll just see how we're both feeling about it."

"So you might carry on seeing him?"

Owen thought about Nathan. His sweet nature, his gentle humour. He couldn't imagine saying goodbye to him at the end of the five dates. "I can think of worse things," he admitted. "But he might not want to keep going out with me."

Owen frowned. Although surely Nathan would — wouldn't he? After all, Nathan was the one who'd insisted on something more meaningful than a casual shag.

"Worried you won't live up his expectations?" Simon teased. "All that build-up.... Five dates of foreplay. You'd better make sure you're not a disappointment."

"My skills are legendary," Owen bragged.

But it was true. He did pride himself on being good at sex. He'd never had any complaints, and if the number of hopeful requests for his contact details after one-night stands were anything to go by, he was doing something right at least. However, the thought of sex with Nathan made him feel oddly nervous. What if they didn't click, or they weren't compatible sexually? No. It didn't bear thinking about. He remembered the fire that Nathan could light in him with his kisses — there was no way it wasn't going to work for them in bed. Speaking of which... he reckoned it was about time to make that phone call.

After a quick shower, Owen got into bed naked. He reached for his phone from the nightstand and sent Nathan a text.

You okay to talk?

I'll call you in five came the reply.

While he waited Owen let his mind drift, imagining Nathan naked.

He bet Nathan had a great body. His arse had looked damn good in those shorts he'd been wearing earlier, and he had lovely broad shoulders and long legs. Owen sighed, spreading his legs under the covers and feeling his hardening cock brush against the cotton. He ran his hands over his chest, skimming the sprinkling of hair, and brushed his fingertips over his nipples. He resisted the urge to reach for his cock. If he started without Nathan it would be game over far too soon.

When his phone finally rang, it felt like he'd been waiting fifteen rather than five minutes. Owen answered it with indecent haste. "Hi."

He swallowed, feeling oddly shy all of a sudden.

"Hi," Nathan replied cautiously. There was a pause. "Did you want something?"

"Well...." Owen deliberately lowered his tone and tried not to laugh as he put on his best sexy voice. "I have this problem I was hoping you could help me with.... " His voice wavered and cracked, and a snort of laughter burst out of him. "Oh, fuck it. I'm sorry. I thought I'd be better at this."

Nathan chuckled. "Very smooth. You mean you haven't had phone sex before? Somehow I thought you'd be an expert."

"No," Owen admitted. "I'm better face-to-face, or face-to-dick — or arse. But I figured it was worth a try because I'm so fucking horny, and I think it could be hot if we can manage it without giggling. What do you reckon — do you want to try it?"

"Yeah, all right," Nathan said. "I'm not sure what to say, though. Everything I think of sounds cheesy."

"Tell me about it. But never mind. Let's just go for it. If I tell you I'm already naked, does it help?"

"Really?" Nathan sounded interested. "You were pretty confident I was going to say yes then?"

"Well, even if you weren't up for it, I was going to have a wank after talking to you anyway. I keep thinking about kissing you and how it felt when you pushed me up against that tree."

"Yeah?"

Encouraged, Owen continued, getting into his stride. He let his free hand trail down his body as he spoke and curled his hand loosely around his cock, stroking lightly at first. "Yeah. I could feel you were hard, and I wanted to suck you so badly. I want to see your cock… feel it in my mouth… taste you." He paused, wondering if Nathan might want a turn to speak.

"Don't stop." Nathan's voice was a little muffled, and Owen could hear the sounds of rustling and what might be a zip being undone. "Oh, fuck." There was a thump and his voice sounded farther away. "Gimme a sec." More rustling and sounds of movement, then Nathan was back, his voice loud and clear again. "There, that's better."

"Dropped the phone?"

"Yeah, I was trying to get some clothes off without putting you down, but I'm sorted now. So tell me more."

"I've lost my flow." Owen stroked his cock a little harder. "Are you naked?"

"Mostly," Nathan replied. "Would it ruin it for you if I told you I still had my socks on? I was impatient."

Owen laughed. "Nah, it's kind of cute. I like that you were in a hurry to get back to me. What are you doing? Are you touching yourself yet?"

"Yes." Nathan sounded slightly breathless now.

"Me too. I'm doing it slowly, though— otherwise I'll come too soon. What are you doing?"

"I'm… uh… I'm touching my arse. Not like actual fingering, just stroking around."

The slightly embarrassed admission sent a jolt of heat through Owen, and he tightened his grip on his cock, thumbing over the head with his next stroke.

"Fuck, really? That's hot. So do you like to bottom?"

"Yeah. Well, I like both. But yeah, I like being fucked."

Owen thrust up into the grip of his fist and did his best porn-star moan without even trying. "I'd fuck you so good," he managed. The challenge with phone sex was going to be staying coherent long enough to get each other off. "God, I'm close already, thinking about that. Tell me what you're doing now. Are you gonna put your fingers in?"

There was a wet sucking sound that made Owen's toes curl.

"Just making them wet..." and then a huff of breath and a grunt.

Owen stilled his hand, listening intently, imagining Nathan with his legs spread and his fingers inside himself.

"Fuck," Nathan gasped. "Should have used lube instead of spit, but it's good anyway."

"Oh my God, Nathan." Owen started moving again, stroking himself, fast and furious. "You're going to make me come. Wish it was me, my cock inside you, fucking you...."

His orgasm was approaching, the tension curling tight, his muscles clenching. Nathan made a broken noise, and it tipped Owen over. He groaned loudly, arching as he came, shooting hard on his belly and chest. A few errant drops even made it as far as his chin, narrowly missing the phone he still had clamped to his ear.

"Holy shit," he muttered weakly when he had enough breath.

"Good?" Nathan's voice was warm and soft in his ear.

"Really fucking good. I nearly jizzed on my bloody phone, though."

Nathan chuckled.

"Did you come yet?" Owen asked.

"Not like this. I need an extra hand for my dick."

"Can you put me on speaker?" Owen suggested.

"Good idea, hold on a sec. There."

"Okay." Now the flush of Owen's orgasm had passed, he felt self-conscious, lying naked and sticky on his bed with Nathan on the other end of the phone. But Nathan's words had got him off, and Owen was determined to return the favour. "So are you still fingering yourself?"

"Yeah," Nathan replied. Owen could hear the rustle of movement as well as his voice.

"If I get to blow you, I could finger you while I do it. Do you like that? A finger in your arse while someone sucks your dick?"

"Fuck, yeah." Nathan sounded desperate now.

Owen figured he wouldn't need much more to get him there. "Or maybe I could eat you out while I play with your cock, drive you crazy with my tongue until you're begging to be fucked. Do you like being rimmed?"

There was a pause, but Owen could still hear the sound of movement and the huff of Nathan's breaths. His voice was hoarse when he finally replied.

"Uh... nobody's ever done that to me. But I think I'd like it."

"Oh, babe. You love arse play and no one's ever rimmed you? You're missing out. It feels amazing. I'd do it for you, lick your hole and jerk you off. You'd come so fucking hard."

"Oh, *God*," Nathan groaned. "Fuck, Owen."

"Yeah, are you coming for me?"

This phone sex lark was way more fun than Owen had expected. His dick had barely softened since he'd come, and the sound of Nathan falling apart and gasping his name had him wondering if he could go for round two.

There was another stifled moan at Nathan's end, and then the sound of ragged breathing, before a shaky voice finally said, "Bollocks. I actually did get jizz on my phone."

They both cracked up laughing, and the mood was broken, but in a good way.

They stayed on the line while they cleaned up a little. Owen pulled on a pair of boxers and got back into bed with his phone pressed back to his ear again.

"That was fucking hot," he admitted. "I wasn't sure I'd like phone sex, but it was fun. I'd still rather be in bed with you, though. I wish I'd been

114

able to see you." And smell you, he thought, but he didn't say it because it sounded a little weird.

"Same."

"Same which? It was hot, or you wish I was there with you?"

"Both, I suppose," Nathan said.

"Why exactly are we waiting again?" Owen kept his voice light and teasing. He didn't want to spoil the moment this time.

"I don't know. I suppose I'm just stubborn. It's only two more weeks anyway."

"And then I can do all the things we talked about?"

"Maybe." Nathan yawned.

"Are you tired? Want me to let you sleep?"

"Soon, don't go yet, though."

There was a rustle of bedcovers. Owen imagined Nathan lying in his bed alone and was shot through with the desire to be there with him now, to be able to trade lazy kisses before settling down to sleep together. *What the fuck?* Owen rarely spent the night with anyone. He hated dealing with the morning after a hookup, it wasn't usually worth the awkwardness for the chance of an extra blowjob. But waking up with Nathan would be different.

"You still there?"

Nathan's voice jolted Owen out of his disturbing train of thought. "Yeah." Owen was feeling sleepy now too. "Yeah, but I'm going to doze off soon."

"Okay, maybe we should hang up." Nathan yawned again. "Sleep well."

"You too." Owen smiled.

"And thanks for today. It was good. All of it."

"Yeah. Yeah, it really was. 'Night, Nathan."

"'Night."

Owen took the phone away from his ear and watched until he saw the call disconnect, then set his phone aside, turned off the light, and rolled onto his side, still smiling as he drifted into sleep.

They kept in touch during the week, mostly by text, but with the occasional call too. On Friday night, Nathan called late, and that time he was the one to suggest they had phone sex.

It was just as much fun as the first time, and after, they lay and chatted for a while.

"I'm not sure if it's going to be easier or harder seeing you tomorrow after doing this," Owen said. "It feels weird that I can talk about sucking your cock, but I'm not allowed to touch it." Then he added, "Of course, the rule is technically no orgasms while we're together. So I guess I could suck your cock as long as you didn't come."

Nathan laughed. "Nice try. But that's never going to happen. I'm pretty sure I'll only last about a minute the first time I get my cock in your mouth."

"I should bloody well hope so after five weeks of foreplay."

There was a short pause.

"So," Owen continued. "Are you going to tell me where we're going tomorrow?"

"No. But you need to wear something old and comfortable. A T-shirt and tracksuit bottoms or loose trousers—definitely not skinny jeans."

117

Owen frowned, wondering where the hell Nathan was taking him. Maybe paintballing, or laser quest, or something. "No other clues?"

"Nope." Nathan sounded annoyingly pleased with himself.

"Do you need me to drive us somewhere?" Owen fished, hoping for more information.

"No. I'll come by your place at about half two. Is that okay?"

"Sure."

They talked a little more until they were both yawning, then reluctantly bid each other goodnight.

"See you tomorrow," Owen yawned. "'Night."

"Sweet dreams."

"I like dirty dreams better."

Nathan laughed. "Dirty dreams then. 'Night, Owen."

Owen looked Nathan up and down when he opened the front door. He looked hot, dressed in baggy khakis and a tight-fitting grey T-shirt that showed off the breadth of his chest and his flat stomach. He had a small backpack slung over his shoulders.

"Will I do?" Owen gestured down at himself. His only tracksuit bottoms were seriously skanky, but he'd found some old jeans that were on the loose side and was wearing a T-shirt that had seen better days.

"Perfect. As long as you can bend and stretch okay in those jeans."

Owen raised an eyebrow, then turned his back on Nathan and touched his toes. "Do you want me to do the splits too?"

"Um, no. I'm good."

When he straightened up, Owen was gratified to notice Nathan was a little flushed.

"So where are you taking me, Mr Mysterious?" He shut the front door behind him and fell into step beside Nathan.

"You'll see."

It wasn't till they turned into the street with the large church tower looming at the end of it, that Owen had an inkling where they were going.

"Are you taking me climbing?" he asked.

Nathan glanced at him and smiled uncertainly. "Is that okay? After last weekend with the rock scrambling I thought you'd like it. But we don't have to if you don't like the idea."

"No! I love it. But I've never tried it, so I'll have no clue what I'm doing. And won't I need a harness and stuff?"

"It's okay. I know what I'm doing, and it's pretty straightforward. I can show you what to do, and we can hire anything we need for you at the climbing centre."

Nathan flashed his membership card when they arrived and insisted on paying for both of them as well as hiring a harness and some climbing shoes for Owen. They both had to sign some paperwork to allow Owen in as a guest.

"I'm in charge of you, so behave." Nathan nudged Owen gently. "No falling off and hurting yourself."

"Aren't you supposed to catch me if I fall anyway?" Owen felt a spike of nervous anticipation. He craned his neck to look up at the plywood walls that soared up into the rafters of the old church. He watched as a climber descended, swinging spider-like on the end of a worryingly thin-looking rope, and his stomach lurched.

"Of course. If you slip off the wall, you won't go far," Nathan assured him.

They went upstairs to change their shoes and leave anything they didn't need in a locker. Nathan made sure Owen's pockets were empty. "If your phone falls out while you're climbing and hits me on the head, it would ruin our date."

Owen met his gaze and stared, distracted by Nathan's blue eyes for a moment. "Yeah, we don't want that."

He went back to fastening his harness with fingers that were sweaty with nerves. Once he was strapped in, Nathan tucked a finger in one of the loops and pulled Owen close. The movement surprised Owen, and he put a hand on Nathan's shoulder for support as Nathan bent and tugged on the straps, tightening and adjusting till he was satisfied with the fit.

"It's quite flattering, isn't it?" Owen thrust his crotch suggestively. The cut of the harness certainly enhanced his package. "Maybe I should get one of these to go clubbing in. It shows off my assets."

Nathan straightened up and chuckled. "But you don't want to get a hard-on in one of these, believe me. So stop waving your dick in my face." He patted Owen on the arse. "You're all set. Let's go."

Nathan insisted Owen climbed first. He picked an easy route, taught Owen the correct knot to tie himself onto one end of the rope that dangled from the top of the wall and did something complicated with the other end through a bit of kit attached to his harness.

"What's that, then?" Owen watched Nathan's hands as he deftly sorted out his end of the rope.

"It's a belay device," Nathan explained. "It creates friction so it's easy for me to catch you if you fall. I'll show you how to do it later, so I can climb too. As long as I always keep one hand on the rope, you're safe. Okay, you're good to go."

Owen looked at the wall stretching up in front of him. It suddenly looked awfully tall.

"So I just climb?"

"Yes, and I'll pull the rope in as you go. So if you slip off—which you won't because this route is almost as easy as climbing a ladder—you won't go far."

"Okay."

Fear and adrenaline made Owen climb fast. Nathan was right—it wasn't difficult at all. But it was new to Owen, and as he hauled himself up on the brightly coloured holds, his heart pounded and his breathing came fast. He faltered for a moment, about halfway up, and looked down to see where his right foot needed to go next.

"Bloody hell." The floor seemed a very long way away. But then his gaze fixed on Nathan who was staring up at him, a huge grin on his face.

"You're doing great, keep going. Get that foot up."

Owen shifted his weight more onto his left hand and lifted his leg, the hold was up near his thigh and awkward to reach. Now he knew why Nathan had told him not to wear skinny jeans.

"Enjoying the view?" He called down to Nathan, wondering what he looked like from below.

"Focus, Owen!" Nathan replied with a chuckle. "But yes."

Owen tilted his head back, fixed his gaze upwards, and went for it. He climbed easily to the top of the wall, slapping the ceiling with the palm of his hand in triumph. "Now what?" he called.

"Now let go, and I'll lower you down."

Owen's stomach lurched at the thought of releasing his grip on the holds. Even though he knew Nathan wouldn't let him fall, it went against every instinct to uncurl his fingers and let his full weight rest in the harness that supported him.

But he trusted Nathan, so he did it.

"Okay," he glanced down over his shoulder. Then "Jesus!" he yelped as he dropped smoothly and steadily but alarmingly quickly. He swung in towards the wall.

"Keep your feet out," Nathan instructed.

Owen pushed off the wall and swung back, then pushed away again, like he'd seen abseilers do. "Hey, this is awesome!"

As he reached the floor, he got both feet under him and managed a graceful landing. He grinned at Nathan, elated and buzzing with adrenaline. "That was brilliant."

Nathan smiled back. "You did great. I knew you'd be a natural. Do you want to do another one?"

"It's your turn next." Owen started to undo the knot that held him onto the rope. "Tell me what I need to do to belay you."

As Owen hadn't done it before, Nathan asked a bloke who worked there to talk Owen through it the first time. "You're supposed to do a course really," Nathan said. "But Ian can show you what to do, and it's not rocket science. As long as you keep a hand on the rope at all times you can't go too far wrong. You take in as I climb, and then lower me down when I get to the top."

Ian was more than happy to keep an eye on Owen while Nathan climbed a couple of routes. Owen managed fine — despite being a little distracted by the perfection of Nathan's arse framed by his harness — and Ian pronounced him competent.

After that they took turns climbing routes, gradually increasing the difficulty. As the afternoon progressed, it was getting hot inside the building. The back door was open, letting in a breeze, but soon they were both sweating with the exertion. While he was climbing up a particularly steep section of wall, Owen glanced to the side and noticed another guy climbing a little to his right, just wearing a pair of shorts. As soon as Owen got back down, he stripped his T-shirt off. If shirtlessness was acceptable, then he was damned if he was going to carry on wearing it.

"That's better." He balled up his shirt and left it at the bottom of the route next to the water bottle they were sharing. "What?" He turned to Nathan who was staring at him. Nathan's gaze raked over Owen's chest, and Owen flushed at the attention. He lowered his voice. "Stop looking at me like that, or this harness is going to get a lot more uncomfortable than it already is."

He turned his attention to untying the knot while Nathan unclipped the belay device from his harness. It was Nathan's turn to climb next and he led the way along the wall to a steeper section where a large overhang jutted out near the top of the route.

"I'm going to try the orange route."

Nathan studied the labels at the foot of the wall where the different routes were colour-coded. The orange was much harder than anything Nathan had attempted so far, with smaller holds that looked few and far between as Owen tried to see where they went.

"Rather you than me."

"It's bloody hot in here. You've got the right idea." Nathan said. Then with one swift movement, he pulled his T-shirt up and over his head.

Owen stared. Nathan's body was even better than he'd imagined. Strong and muscular with a smattering of gold chest hair that was almost invisible until it caught the light. His skin was pale apart from where his cheeks and throat were flushed from the heat. Owen wanted to pin him up against the wall and suck marks onto his chest.

Nathan cleared his throat, and Owen raised his eyes to meet an amused smirk.

"You ready for me to climb?" Nathan raised his eyebrows.

"Uh… yeah, sure," Owen managed, taking in the slack on the rope and trying not to let his gaze drop again.

He turned, moving in to stand behind Nathan as he faced the wall, ready to climb. Owen breathed in and caught the scent of warm skin and sweat, and it was all he could do not to move closer and touch.

As Nathan climbed, Owen watched the play of muscles in his back and the curve of his arse. Nathan moved gracefully for such a big guy, all fluid movements as he scaled the wall. He paused at the overhang, balancing on his feet as he looked up assessingly.

"Get on with it!" Owen teased, trying to break the spell Nathan had cast on him.

"Just working out what I need to do. It looks like a bitch of a move."

Nathan went for it, climbing under the plywood shelf until he was almost horizontal. He hesitated for a moment, then hauled himself round with a grunt of effort that made Owen's mind go to very dirty places. Owen took in the slack on the rope quickly as Nathan made short work of the top section of wall, whooping in triumph as he finally reached the ceiling.

Nathan let go with no warning, the sudden weight of him nearly jerking Owen off the ground. Owen lowered him down, and Nathan was grinning when his feet finally touched the ground.

"Well done." Owen gave him a little more slack, so he could untie.

"Wow, that was hard." Nathan's fingers were trembling as he fumbled with the knot.

"It looked it," Owen replied, then added, "and it sounded it too, if the sex noises were anything to go by."

Nathan's eyes opened wide and his already flushed cheeks got even pinker. "Fuck you."

Owen chuckled. "I wish. Here, let me." He batted Nathan's trembling hands away from the knot he was trying unsuccessfully to loosen. "You're a mess."

"Yeah. My arms are knackered now." Nathan flexed his fingers. "I had nothing left by the time I got to the top. I could hardly hold on."

Owen tugged him a little closer with the rope. He could feel the heat radiating off Nathan's bare skin as he worked the knot loose. "There you go." He raised his eyes to meet Nathan's gaze, holding it for a moment as Nathan stared back.

Nathan licked his lips. "Thanks."

Owen stepped away, before he gave in to the urge to back Nathan up against the wall and snog him senseless. Hopefully there would be opportunities for that later.

"So are we done here?" he asked. "I don't think my arms can take much more, and I'm getting hungry. Did you have a plan for later?"

"How about a beer when we leave here, and then we could get a takeaway and go back to my place?"

"Sounds great."

"We'll have it to ourselves," Nathan added. "Kirsty's gone back home this weekend."

"Even better." Owen grinned.

Back at Nathan's flat, they put some music on and sprawled comfortably on the sofa, sharing the Chinese food they'd picked up on the way home. With one beer inside him from the pub near the climbing centre and another that was washing the food down, Owen was feeling the perfect amount of slightly tipsy. He basked in the warm glow of Nathan's companionship and the residual buzz from the experience of climbing earlier.

"I think today was my favourite date so far," he said as he finally admitted defeat and set his plate aside, no room left for the last bit of chow mein. "Thanks."

Nathan looked pleased with himself. "I'm really glad you enjoyed it. I can't believe you've never tried it before."

"Yeah, I've been missing out. But now I know how cool it is, I'd definitely like to do it again." There was a pause, and Owen suddenly realised how that sounded. He didn't mean to assume Nathan would want to take him there again. "I mean, I might do a course or something, so I can meet other beginners to climb with."

"We can go again together if you want," Nathan offered.

Owen turned sideways on the sofa so he could see him properly, putting his socked feet up so his toes were nearly touching Nathan's leg.

Nathan forked up the last bits of rice on his plate and transferred them to his mouth. "Unless you'd rather climb with someone else."

"Nah." Owen wiggled his toes closer, tucking them under Nathan's thigh. "I like the view when

I'm climbing with you." He let his voice drip with suggestion.

"Yeah?" Nathan put his plate on the coffee table and reached for Owen's ankle, circling it with a firm grip.

"Mm-hmm." A smile tugged at Owen's lips.

Nathan moved, knocking Owen's thighs apart so he could fit between them as he lowered his body and found Owen's mouth with his own. Owen kissed him back, enjoying the warm weight of Nathan on top of him. He slid one hand into Nathan's hair to keep him there and worked his other one up the back of Nathan's shirt, hot skin against his palm and the shift of lean muscle.

This was the first time they'd been alone like this, somewhere safe with no fear of interruption, and Owen gave himself up to the sensations, heat and desperation building fast. Nathan ground down against him, and Owen arched up, rubbing his erection against the bulge of Nathan's. It would be shockingly easy to come like this, he suddenly realised, and he knew they should slow things down. Not because he didn't want this. He wanted

Nathan badly. But he didn't want to do something they might regret later, not when things had been going so well between them.

He turned his head, tearing his lips away from Nathan's hungry kisses. "Nathan," he gasped, voice husky.

But Nathan carried on, his lips and tongue burning a hot wet trail down Owen's neck.

"*Nathan.*" Owen tugged on Nathan's hair now, pulling his head up so Owen could see his face. Nathan's mouth was wet and plush, his eyes glazed with desire, and the look he gave Owen didn't help one bit.

But they had an agreement.

"If we carry on like this, I'm going to come." Owen held Nathan's gaze as he spelled it out, the warning clear.

Nathan stared back at him, his expression unreadable as the moment stretched out. Owen was torn, desperately wanting to pull him back down and pick up where they'd left off. But he didn't want that unless Nathan was sure, so he waited, his body taut, fingers curled tight in Nathan's hair.

Nathan swallowed. "Yeah, me too."

He drew back from Owen's grip and pushed up to stand beside the sofa, adjusting his erection through his trousers.

Owen bit back a groan and tried to hide his disappointment, cursing himself for putting the brakes on. Since when had he developed a conscience? But then Nathan held out a hand. Owen frowned, searching Nathan's face for an explanation as Nathan stood there waiting.

"If we're going to come, I want to do it without all these fucking clothes in the way," Nathan said gruffly. "My bedroom?"

Owen's heart surged. "You sure? Unless I've counted wrong, this is only date four."

Nathan shrugged, his lips twisting in a small grin. "I'm tired of waiting."

A heady mixture of relief and arousal flooded through Owen, and he grinned back, finally taking Nathan's hand and letting Nathan pull him up. "Oh, thank fuck for that. Me too."

Chapter Six

Nathan's head whirled as he laced their fingers together and led Owen to his room.

He was aware he was thinking with his dick rather than his brain at this point, but he didn't care. He was crazy about Owen, and he didn't want to wait any more. He didn't see the benefit in hanging on for another week. It wasn't like there was a bet to lose. Sure — they'd made an agreement, but so what? He wanted Owen, Owen wanted him back, and the moment felt right. They knew each other now. There was a connection between them that would make this more than casual sex, whatever happened after. And right now Nathan didn't care about the future. He just wanted to get naked with Owen and make each other come.

Nathan kicked the door shut behind them and switched on the lamp by the bed, still holding

Owen's hand. Then they kissed again, hands fumbling with each other's clothes as they did their best to undress without breaking contact. Owen gasped in a shocked breath as Nathan got his hand around Owen's cock, and Nathan chuckled. They kissed some more, punctuated by T-shirts coming off and Owen pausing to swear about Nathan's fiddly button fly.

Once they were both naked, Nathan dropped to his knees and pressed teasing kisses all over Owen's belly and the tops of his muscular thighs. Owen wound his fingers in Nathan's hair and stroked his scalp, his hips flexing as his cock bobbed, warm and silky against Nathan's cheek. He was wet and glistening at the tip, and Nathan wanted to taste him, but he couldn't resist prolonging the moment, sensing Owen's desperation and enjoying the teasing.

When Owen moaned aloud, Nathan finally gave in, capturing the head of his cock between his lips and sucking him in, slowly, his gaze fixed on Owen, who had his head back and eyes closed, mouth slack with pleasure.

137

"Oh, fuck," Owen breathed.

Nathan swirled his tongue, and the taste of precome made his mouth water. He used the slickness to take Owen deeper until he felt Owen nudge the back of his throat. Then he slid his mouth up and down lazily, keeping it slow.

Owen cupped Nathan's face with one of his hands and opened his eyes to watch, tugging gently on Nathan's hair with the other. "So fucking good. You look so sexy."

Nathan hummed around his mouthful of dick to encourage Owen and brought one hand down to stroke himself where he was hard and aching to be touched. He noticed Owen's eyes track the movement, and Owen moaned again as he watched Nathan fist his cock.

Nathan took him deeper, sucking harder. Owen felt so good in his mouth, hot and hard, the taste and scent of him filling Nathan's senses. Lost in the pleasure of it, Nathan closed his eyes and drifted until Owen backed off, pulling out of Nathan's mouth. Owen swiped Nathan's lower lip with the pad of his thumb, wiping away the sticky drool that had collected at the corners of his mouth.

"I don't want to come yet," Owen told him. "Let me suck you for a bit."

He held out a hand to Nathan and pulled him up, then guided him to the bed. They lay down together, kissing, hands stroking each other's bodies, and Owen rolled Nathan onto his back. His eyes raked over Nathan possessively.

"In your own time," Nathan teased, thrusting up, so his cock pressed against Owen's arse where he straddled his hips.

"I'm not sure about this," Owen said, mock seriously. "Maybe we should wait another week." He rocked down against Nathan, moving his hips in a slow, dirty grind.

"Fucker."

Nathan gripped Owen's waist and thrust up against him as Owen leaned down for a kiss. Their cocks slid together, wet and sticky.

Owen teased Nathan as he slowly moved down the bed. His body brushed Nathan's cock as he worked his way down, kissing and stroking

Nathan everywhere. He murmured constantly about how gorgeous Nathan was, how much he wanted him. He focused on Nathan's nipples for ages when he realised how sensitive they were, licking and sucking on them until Nathan wanted to scream at him to hurry the fuck up and suck his dick already.

"Owen," he whined instead, arching his hips up hopefully and pushing Owen's fringe out of his eyes so he could see him properly.

"Hmm?" Owen gazed up at him, expression mischievous as he circled Nathan's nipple with his tongue, then sucked a red mark just below it.

"You said something about sucking me?"

Owen grinned. "I don't think I specified which bit."

But he slid down the bed and finally got his mouth where Nathan wanted it.

"After all that fucking teasing" — Nathan gasped, digging his fingers into the mattress — "you're not actually going to get to suck it for long. Jesus."

Owen wasn't teasing now. He worked Nathan over with his hand at the base of Nathan's cock, driving Nathan rapidly towards the point of no return with perfect suction and tantalising swipes of his tongue.

Nathan moved his hands into Owen's hair, tangling them in the dark strands. "I'm going to come," he gasped out a warning, unsure whether Owen would want to swallow.

But Owen carried on the rhythm he'd set, moaning around Nathan's cock as Nathan came.

Nathan's whole body locked up tight as he jerked and spilled into Owen's mouth. His fingers clenched reflexively in Owen's hair, holding him still as Nathan thrust up into that slick heat and let the waves of pleasure wash over him. He finally collapsed back, breathless and limp. Owen pulled off and knelt up, straddling Nathan's thighs. His gaze was hot and hungry as it swept over him. Owen took his cock in hand and pumped it.

"What do you want me to do?" Nathan asked. He wasn't sure he could get it together to move much right now, but Owen could fuck his mouth right where he was. Nathan would be down for that.

"This is good." Owen stroked himself faster.

Nathan lay back and watched. It was like his own personal live porn show. Owen looked debauched, all flushed and sweaty. Owen pinched his nipples with his free hand and made a needy sound. Nathan reached for Owen's balls, cupping and rubbing them, feeling them draw up in his hand.

"Fuck, yeah…" Owen threw his head back and bit down on his lip.

His hips stuttered, fucking into the grip of his fist as he came, spurting thick, warm stripes all over Nathan's cock and belly.

Owen chuckled as he squeezed out the last few drops. "Look at the state of you."

Nathan stretched luxuriously and smiled. "Totally worth it."

Owen chuckled, lowering himself down for a kiss with his arms on either side of Nathan's head. "Yeah, definitely. And worth waiting for too."

His lips were soft and gentle as they parted against Nathan's, and Nathan wanted to pull him down and hold him for a while. But Owen rolled off him asking, "Where's your bathroom? I'll get you a cloth."

"Next door."

Owen came back a couple of minutes later with a wet flannel. Owen pulled his underwear back on and sat on the edge of the bed as Nathan cleaned up a little, then drew the duvet back up to cover himself. He avoided Owen's eyes, feeling awkward now the intimacy of the sex had passed and unsure of where he stood. Owen didn't say anything either, and Nathan wondered if he was feeling uncomfortable too.

Desperate for reassurance but not sure how to ask for it, Nathan tried to lighten the mood.

"Well, I guess that's it, then," he joked, "You'll be on your way now you've got what you wanted."

Owen snapped his head round, confusion on his features. "What the fuck's that supposed to mean?" His voice was sharp and angry.

Nathan backpedalled quickly, propping up on his elbows as he tried to explain. "I was just kidding… well, sort of." The lurch of adrenaline that ripped through him now he realised he'd said the wrong thing made it hard for him to collect his thoughts. "Only… you know. This is date four, and we didn't hold out. So I guess we won't be needing a fifth."

"I guess not if that's how you feel about it." Owen sounded stiff and hurt. He got off the bed, stooped to pick up his clothes, and started to pull them on. "I'll get out of your hair, then."

"Owen, that's not what I—"

But Owen wasn't listening, "I didn't realise your opinion of me was *quite* that low. Jesus Christ, Nathan. Did you seriously think I was only going out with you to get in your pants? I mean, sure, I wanted to bang you. It wasn't a secret. But I tried really hard here. We got to know each other. We bonded and stuff. I did everything you asked me to. And anyway, it's not like I even got to fuck you yet, so if you think I'm that much of a wanker, surely you'd be expecting me to take you out again next weekend, just so I can have your arse as well as your mouth?"

He tripped as he tried to slip his feet into his trainers without undoing the laces and cursed as he stumbled. He shoved his feet into them viciously, squashing the backs down.

"But I didn't mean—" Nathan tried.

Owen interrupted him again. "This was your bloody idea anyway. *You* were the one who didn't want to wait today. Not me. I tried to put the brakes on, remember?"

Before Nathan could get another word in, Owen was gone, and Nathan was left naked and stunned by Owen's outburst.

"But I was only joking," he said to the door that Owen had slammed shut behind him. Then he raised his voice. "*I was only fucking joking!*"

His only answer was the muffled thud of the front door in the distance.

"Bollocks."

Nathan flopped back onto the mattress and rubbed his face with his hands. He appeared to have fucked things up spectacularly. Anger surged through him, directed at himself but also at Owen. Stroppy bastard, flying off the handle without giving Nathan time to explain. Nathan hadn't seen that side of Owen before — who knew he had such a temper? Well fuck him — metaphorically speaking.

Nathan got up and showered, scrubbing the last traces of Owen off his skin. He stayed in there for ages, letting the water pound into his shoulders and the back of his neck until it started to run cool.

Once he'd dried and dressed, he got his phone and threw himself down on the sofa, still tense and angry. He glared at the screen for a few moments before typing the words that Owen hadn't given him a chance to say before he stormed off.

I was only fucking joking

He refused to apologise now, not when Owen hadn't let him speak earlier. Even though Nathan knew that part of the fault lay with him, Owen's reaction had been completely out of proportion. If he'd shut up and let Nathan explain, then all this could have been avoided.

Not waiting for a reply, he switched off his phone and turned on the TV, flicking through the channels until he found some action movie with lots of guns and explosions. He didn't give a shit about the plot, but it suited his mood, so he watched it until his eyelids started to droop and then dragged himself to bed. As he rolled onto his side and tucked his hand under the pillow, he caught the faint scent of Owen's shampoo on his pillowcase. Sighing, he turned the pillow over and squeezed his eyes closed. His anger had subsided, leaving a hollow feeling in his chest.

He didn't want to think about Owen, he just wanted to sleep.

The cool night air calmed Owen's anger a little on the walk home but did nothing to soothe the hurt that had settled in his stomach like a cold, heavy stone.

Fuck.

Did Nathan really think so little of him, after all the time they'd spent together? Owen thought he'd managed to show Nathan he was serious about him. But it seemed Nathan had taken Owen at face value, just like everyone else. Good old Owen — a bit of a tart, good for a laugh, but not for anything meaningful. But this time things had been different, or Owen had thought they were.

He nearly tripped over an empty Coke can that someone had left lying on the pavement, and he stamped on it savagely, crushing it almost flat, then kicked it as hard as he could. It rattled off into the darkness under a parked car. Owen wished he could make his feelings disappear as easily.

Back at the flat, he was hoping he could sneak off to his room to lick his wounds in peace. But no such luck. He bumped into Simon in the hallway as he came in.

Simon smiled. "Oh hi, Owen. How was the date?" But then he registered Owen's expression, and his face fell. "Oh, pet. What's up?"

Owen shook his head. "I don't want to talk about it."

He should have known Simon wouldn't take no for an answer. He took Owen's elbow, steering him firmly into the living room where Jack was watching TV. Jack took one look at Owen's face and paused the show.

Simon pushed Owen down onto the sofa next to Jack and sat down on his other side, one hand on Owen's knee.

"Do you want me to go?" Jack asked.

Even though he'd been living there a while now and was as much Owen's friend as Simon was, he still tended to defer to Simon's best-friend status in times of crisis.

Owen shook his head. "No, it's fine. I know Simon will tell you everything anyway. And knowing him, he'll probably exaggerate."

Simon pouted as Jack chuckled.

"It's no big deal," Owen said. "We just had a bit of a falling-out."

There was a silence. It was obvious neither of the others were going to fill it. So Owen sighed. "It's stupid, really, and I probably overreacted, but he touched a nerve."

Simon squeezed Owen's knee. "What happened?"

149

"We had a great date. It all went well, and I went back to his place. Then stuff happened," Owen waved a hand vaguely.

"Sex stuff?" Simon asked. "I *knew* you wouldn't make it to five dates. That's a tenner you owe me," he addressed Jack over Owen's head.

Owen glared at him.

"Oh, sorry. You were saying?" Simon has the decency to look slightly guilty.

"So after, Nathan made some comment about how I might as well go now I'd got what I wanted."

"Ouch." Jack winced.

"Seriously?" Simon's voice raised in anger. "What a fucker. I can't believe he said that."

"Well, the thing is, now I've calmed down a bit, I think maybe he was joking," Owen admitted. "But at the time I was really angry and didn't let him explain."

"Ugh," Simon said. "That sucks."

"Yeah."

"It was a shitty thing to say, though, even if he *was* joking," Jack said. "Especially straight after sex."

"Yeah," Owen said again, then sighed.

His phone buzzed in his pocket, breaking the silence.

"That might be him, apologising," Simon suggested. "Well, go on, aren't you going to look?"

Owen pulled his phone out.

"'I was only fucking joking,'" he read out the words on the screen. "Not much of an apology, is it? Fuck it. I'm going to bed."

He stood, and Simon's hand fell away from his knee.

"Aren't you gonna reply?" Jack asked.

"Not tonight. I've got a headache." Owen attempted to joke, but he knew it was weak. He was still hurting, and Nathan's text had rekindled his anger. "I'm going to crash and sleep on it."

He brushed his teeth so hard, he made his gums bleed, then stripped down to his boxers and got into bed. He read Nathan's message again, then turned off his phone and tried to sleep. But he tossed and turned, unable to settle. His thoughts wouldn't switch off, and the horrible, hollow feeling in his gut persisted.

Eventually he turned his phone back on and typed a reply:

You need to work on your jokes, it wasn't funny :(

Owen waited awhile to see whether Nathan would text back, but after half an hour, he gave up. He was buggered if he was going to wait up all night for an apology. He switched off his phone again so that he wouldn't be listening for it and forced himself into sleep with a combination of brutal determination, deep breathing, and sheep counting.

He refused to lose sleep over one stupid comment.

Nathan slept surprisingly well, considering.

He woke late in the morning feeling rested and relaxed. Still half asleep, he rolled onto his back and stretched luxuriously. He let his hand creep down to squeeze his morning erection and weighed his options between having a wank in bed now or in the shower a little later. But then the events of the evening before came flooding back into his consciousness in a cold, unpleasant rush, dousing his libido as effectively as a bucket of icy water.

"Fuck," he muttered.

He got up and made a bowl of cereal, eating mechanically as his mind replayed the stupid argument he'd had with Owen. When he finished he found his phone on the coffee table where he'd left it last night and turned it back on.

There was a reply from Owen about an hour after Nathan had texted him.

You need to work on your jokes, it wasn't funny :(

The sad face hit Nathan like a punch in the gut. He knew his flippant comment had pissed Owen off, but he hadn't really made the connection that he'd hurt him. He definitely owed Owen an apology.

He was tempted to text, unsure how Owen was going to react, but texts could be misconstrued or the tone misinterpreted, and Nathan felt they'd already fucked up their communication enough for one weekend. So he plucked up his courage and pressed Call.

It rang and rang, then went to voice mail. "Shit," Nathan cursed as he listened to Owen's recorded message. His heart thumped uncomfortably, but he didn't end the call.

"Um… it's me. I'm sorry for making that stupid comment. Can you call me? I really want to talk to you."

He lay back on the sofa, phone in hand, and waited.

Just as he was about to give up and go and find something to do as a distraction, his phone buzzed, and his adrenaline surged as he saw Owen's name on the screen.

"Hi, thanks for calling back." Nathan gripped the phone tightly, staring at a damp patch on the ceiling.

"Sorry it took a while. I was in the shower."

There was a long pause while Nathan tried to find the right words, but before he could shape a coherent sentence, Owen filled the silence by saying, "It *was* a stupid comment."

Nathan snorted. "You got my message, then. Yeah… I really am sorry. It was a stupid thing to say, but I honestly didn't mean you to take it seriously."

There was an uncomfortable pause before Owen finally replied. "I thought you meant it…." The raw honesty in his voice cut through Nathan. "That you thought you were still only a conquest to me."

"I don't know what I am to you," Nathan said honestly. "I still don't."

There was a huff of breath on the end of the line. "Yeah, okay. I'm not sure I know yet either. But you're definitely more than a casual hookup, that's for sure. I like you—a lot—and I don't want this to be over yet."

Nathan's chest expanded with relief. "Me too. So, do you forgive me for being a twat?"

"I suppose," Owen's voice was light, obviously teasing. But then he sounded serious again as he admitted, "And I guess I did overreact a tad…."

155

"Just a tad," Nathan agreed, trying not to chuckle.

"It's my Welsh temper. We're fiery, you know — like the dragon on our flag," Owen told him. "Or, okay, maybe that's a bullshit excuse, but I'm sorry I didn't give you time to explain last night."

"It's okay. We're good now, yeah?"

"Yeah."

"So, are we back on for the fifth date?" Nathan asked, crossing the fingers of his free hand as he waited for Owen's reply.

"Of course."

"Good. I want to make it up to you for ruining things last night, so I'll text or call you and let you know what we're doing once I've worked it out. But keep Saturday evening free."

He didn't have a plan in mind, but he knew he wanted to make it special.

"Okay."

The silence stretched out, but it wasn't awkward like before. Nathan couldn't think of anything to say. He wished Owen were there so they could kiss and make up, but it would have to wait till next week. He sighed. "I guess I'd better go. I was going to head to the gym before lunch."

"Nice. I'll imagine you all sweaty and pumped while I'm lying on the sofa in my pyjamas."

"Lazy."

"Yeah, well. My shoulders are killing me after climbing yesterday, so I'm not doing anything energetic today."

"Aw, poor baby. You need a massage," Nathan teased.

"Are you offering?"

Nathan considered it for a moment. The thought of sacking his plans for the day and getting his hands all over Owen instead was tempting.

But Owen cut in again before he could answer. "Don't worry. I've got loads of shit I need to do today, and if you came over here, I wouldn't get any of it done."

"Next Saturday, then?"

"Yeah, next Saturday. But we'll speak before then?"

"Sure."

157

When they ended the call, Nathan grinned at the ceiling, his mind already running over some possible plans for their next date.

They talked on the phone every night that week before they went to sleep.

It wasn't planned; it just happened. One or other of them would call or text... but the texting always ended with a call anyway because they had too much to say, and then they'd talk until one or both of them started yawning and almost dropping off while they were speaking.

Sometimes the calls were flirty and sexy, but other times they chatted about their days, their families, their ambitions, and dreams for the future. They skirted around the subject of their relationship. Nathan had been doing a lot of thinking with the fifth date approaching. He definitely didn't want to end things there, and he was pretty confident Owen didn't either, but neither of them had acknowledged the elephant in the room, and there had been no discussion about what would happen next. Nathan supposed they'd cross that bridge on Saturday.

Meanwhile Nathan had been making plans.

Kirsty was going to be away again — off on a hen weekend this time — so Nathan would have the flat to himself. He wanted to surprise Owen, to plan something special. But in order to do it, he was going to need some help.

He texted Simon on Thursday evening, asking him to call when Owen wasn't around.

"What's up?" Simon asked when he called Nathan a little later. "This is all a bit cloak-and-dagger. Is everything okay? You'd better not have upset my boy again."

"No, everything's fine," Nathan hastily assured him. "But I'm planning something for Saturday, and I need your input. I want to cook for Owen, but I'm not sure what his favourite foods are, and I thought you would know. Is there anything he really hates or is allergic to or anything?"

"Aw, that's cute. Hang on. Let me think… Jack?" Simon's voice sounded a little muffled now as though he was holding the phone away from his face. "What stuff have you cooked that Owen likes?" He addressed Nathan again. "Jack's the one who's into cooking. Before he moved in we ate a lot of sausages and baked beans, and supermarket pizza."

Nathan could hear Jack in the background but he couldn't make out his reply.

"He says you can't go wrong with a nice piece of meat." Simon giggled. "I'm inclined to agree."

"Very funny. Can you be more specific?"

"Oh, just give me the damn phone." Jack's voice was clearer that time.

"Okay, I'm handing you over to my resident meat expert," Simon said, tone dripping with innuendo. "He'll sort you out, won't you, baby?"

"Oh, my God." But Nathan chuckled despite himself.

"I'm sorry about Simon." Nathan could practically hear Jack's eye-roll down the phone. "He can't help himself. But seriously, Owen's a steak man. Medium rare."

"Okay, thanks, Jack. Any suggestions for pudding?"

"Lemon cheesecake," Jack replied promptly. "He sometimes buys those individual ones from the supermarket, so I know he likes them."

"That's brilliant, thanks." Nathan wasn't sure if he had the right stuff in his kitchen to make a cheesecake, but he supposed he could always go to one of the posher supermarkets and buy a good one.

"Simon wants to talk to you again. I hope the date goes well."

Me too, Nathan thought, his stomach fluttering with nerves. It felt like there was an awful lot riding on this last date of the five.

"He really likes you, you know." Simon sounded more serious than Nathan had ever heard him. "I know it's not my business, and I should probably stay out of it—ouch, stop kicking me, Jack—but I've never seen Owen so goofy over anyone before. He was gutted on Saturday night when you had that row and a miserable wanker first thing on Sunday, till you called him."

Nathan flushed, but he was smiling at Simon's words.

"Yeah, well… we sorted it out."

"I gathered that much. Now don't fuck it up again, or I'll have to come round there and kick your arse."

Nathan snorted. "Yeah, right." Simon was six inches shorter than him and approximately half the width.

"I'll get Jack to help, he might not be much bigger than me, but he does tae kwon do, and he could totally take you."

"Okay, Simon, I get it. I won't fuck it up. I really like him too, you know."

"Oh, thank God for that," Simon sighed with relief. "So, yeah, I just wanted you to know. I think Owen's into you even if he's scared of admitting it—Jack's glaring at me, so I'll stop now. Good luck on Saturday."

"Thanks, and um… thanks for telling me."

"You're welcome. Bye, Nathan."

"Bye."

Nathan set his phone aside and grinned like an idiot.

162

Now he needed to make sure everything was perfect on Saturday. He'd better make a shopping list.

It wasn't that Nathan was completely shit at cooking. He could get by, but beans on toast was more his speed than what he had planned for Owen, so he had a lot to research.

The Internet was his friend, and Nathan spent the rest of the evening finding all the information he needed. He googled "how to cook a perfect steak" and printed off the instructions, and he googled for ideas about what to serve *with* the perfect steak once he'd cooked it. Then he searched for lemon cheesecake recipes and narrowed it down to one that wasn't too daunting. After a quick rummage around in the kitchen cupboards, he found a suitable-looking tin to bake it in.

"What the hell are you doing?" Kirsty asked as she came into the kitchen in her pyjamas.

"Finding a tin to bake cheesecake. I think this will do."

"You're making cheesecake when I'm going away for the weekend? You're the worst flatmate ever." She filled the kettle and got out a mug. "Want anything?"

"No, thanks. And I can probably save you a piece. I doubt me and Owen will eat it all."

"You're cooking for him? Nice." She nodded approvingly. "Oh yes, I'd forgotten, but it's the all-important fifth date this weekend, right?" She leaned back against the kitchen cupboards and grinned at him.

"Yes," Nathan admitted.

"No pressure, then. So are you going to finally… you know?"

Nathan's face heated, and he avoided her gaze as he answered. "Maybe."

Nathan hadn't told her about how he'd caved and then nearly messed everything up last weekend. They didn't have the sort of friendship where they told each other too many details, and he'd felt so stupid about it, he'd wanted to keep it to himself.

There was a pause, and Nathan risked a glance at Kirsty and found her watching him assessingly, her eyes narrowed.

"You've already shagged him, haven't you?"

"No!" Nathan protested, but he knew his intensifying blush was giving him away. "Not shagged exactly… just—"

"Okay, okay." She held her hands up. "I don't need details. But I'm assuming you didn't stick to the original terms of the whole five-date thing?"

Nathan shook his head. "Not so much. No."

She smirked. "But you're having a fifth date anyway? Well that's cool, then. Must be a first for Owen. He's probably never even had one date before, let alone five. Nice work, Nathan. I need you to give me lessons on how to keep a man."

"Oh, shut up," Nathan said, rolling his eyes at her. "It's not like that. I didn't go into this with a plan to trap him, you know."

"Well, either way, it seems to have worked." The kettle boiled, and she turned to pour hot water into her mug. "Are you boyfriends now?"

"I don't know. We still haven't discussed what's going to happen after this weekend."

"But you want to be with him?" She still had her back to Nathan, dealing with the teabag.

"Yes." Nathan's gut twisted at the admission, but Owen was lodged under his skin like a splinter, and he didn't see the point in denying it. "I really do."

"Well, he's a lucky guy, then. I hope he's good enough for you." All trace of teasing was gone from her voice now, and her expression was hard to read as she turned, steaming mug in hand. "'Night, Nathan." She passed him, leaving a waft of peppermint in her wake.

"'Night," he called after her. "Sleep well."

Nathan texted Owen late, once he was ready for bed.

Come to mine on Saturday. 7.30

His phone rang immediately, and Nathan smiled when he saw it was Owen.

"Hey," Owen said as soon as Nathan answered. "Are we going out somewhere? Do I need to wear anything in particular?"

"Nope, we're staying in. So you can wear whatever."

"Staying in?"

"Yes. Kirsty's away, and I'm going to make dinner."

"Cool."

They talked for a while until Nathan started to yawn. "I guess I'd better go," he said reluctantly. "I'm knackered."

"Yeah, you need to keep your strength up for Saturday." Owen's voice was dirty.

"Oh, really?"

"Mm-hmm. I've got plans for you." There was a telltale rustle on the other end of the line.

Nathan reached down to squeeze the bulge that was growing in his boxers as he imagined Owen in bed, touching himself. "Are you wanking?"

"Maybe a little."

Nathan chuckled. "Well, I can stay awake a little longer if you like..."

"You'll sleep better after." Owen's voice was a little breathy now.

"So," Nathan pushed his boxers down so that he could grip his cock. "Tell me about these plans."

"Well, remember how you said you'd never had anyone eat you out?"

"Fuck," Nathan moaned. "Why isn't it Saturday tomorrow?"

Owen chuckled. "Not long to wait now."

Nathan planned his day on Saturday like a military operation.

He shopped for ingredients in the morning, then spent the afternoon attempting to bake a lemon cheesecake. It came out of the oven looking pretty much like the one in the photo on the website, so he counted that as a win. He wished he could taste it — what if it was minging? But the combination of ingredients sounded good, so he just had to hope for the best.

While the cheesecake was cooling, Nathan scrubbed new potatoes and topped and tailed green beans, then heated up raspberries with sugar and mashed them through a sieve to make a sauce for the cheesecake.

By the time Nathan was done, the kitchen looked as though a bomb had gone off in it. He spent the next half hour washing up all the things he'd made dirty and sweeping up the sugar and flour he'd managed to sprinkle liberally all over the worktops and the floor.

Once the kitchen was clean again, the cheesecake was cool enough to go in the fridge, and Nathan was hot, bothered, and exhausted — but full of nervous excitement. When he looked at his watch, it was already six o'clock. Where the hell had his afternoon gone?

The kitchen was tidy, but the rest of the flat was still in its usual, rather cluttered state, his sheets needed changing — although he was hoping he'd get to mess them up again later — and the carpets were badly in need of a hoover. Nathan hurried to get all that done and then finally set the table in the small living room with cutlery, wineglasses, side plates, and the dark blue paper napkins and candles he'd bought specially.

Surveying the scene, Nathan smiled in satisfaction. It looked unashamedly romantic and perfect.

He headed for the shower with half an hour to spare.

Chapter Seven

Owen rang the bell and waited on the doorstep. His heart was beating faster than it should be from the walk here. He tightened his grip on the carrier bag he was holding and tried to ignore the swoopy feeling in his stomach.

The door opened, and Nathan's wide smile sent the butterflies tumbling again, but in a good way.

"Hi," Nathan said.

"Hi." Owen grinned back, momentarily blinded by Nathan's gorgeousness, and Nathan stared back at him for a moment that should maybe have been awkward, but just felt sweet.

"Sorry." Nathan shook himself, breaking the spell. "Come in."

He stepped aside to let Owen through the door, and Owen paused to kiss him on the lips as he passed. Nathan smelled of shower gel, and when Owen put a hand on the back of his neck to hold him there, Nathan's hair was still damp where it curled on the collar of his shirt.

"You look good," Owen said as he stepped back, taking in the pale blue shirt that set off the blue of Nathan's eyes and the broad strength of his shoulders.

"So do you." Nathan's gaze roamed over Owen, making Owen feel warm and tingly. Nathan pushed a lock of Owen's hair out of his eyes and kissed him again, a little more insistently this time until they parted, still grinning at each other.

"I thought you were going to feed me first," Owen teased.

"I am. Come on. Let me get you a drink."

He guided Owen to the living room with a hand in the small of his back.

"Wow." Owen stopped and stared at the table and the candles.

"I got a little carried away." Nathan hovered beside him. "It's probably a bit much. I just wanted —"

"No, no, it's great. Really," Owen assured him, touched by the amount of effort Nathan had gone to. "Nobody's ever done anything like this for me before. It's awesome."

"Good." Nathan sounded relieved. "So, do you want a drink? I opened some red wine to breathe, or I've got beer if you'd rather, or something soft?"

"Wine sounds great."

Nathan poured them each a glass, then brought them over to where Owen was still standing.

"So, I need to go and finish cooking the food now," Nathan said. "Do you want to hang out in here? You can watch TV or whatever."

"Can't I come and keep you company? I promise I won't get in the way. Or I can help if you want?"

"There's nothing for you to do, but company's good."

There was nowhere to sit in Nathan's kitchen as it was only small, so Owen leaned against the kitchen counter and sipped his wine, watching Nathan as he turned the gas ring on under a saucepan.

"What are we having?" Owen asked.

"Steaks. Not very imaginative, but hopefully I can't fuck it up."

"No! That's perfect. I love steak."

"I know. Simon told me," Nathan admitted with a smile.

"You did research?"

"Yep." Nathan nodded, flushing and looking pleased with himself.

"No wonder Simon's been grinning and looking knowingly at me all day."

Nathan checked his watch and turned another ring on the cooker under a second pan.

"Are you sure I can't do anything?" Owen asked.

"Really. I've got the potatoes and beans on. There's just the steaks to do now." Nathan reached behind the kitchen door. "Okay, please don't laugh, but this is the only apron in the house."

The apron was pale pink and decorated with cupcakes, and also slightly too small for Nathan. He looked oddly adorable in it as he fumbled to tie the strings behind him.

"I can help with that." Owen stepped forwards and batted his hands away. He tied it deftly in a bow in the small of Nathan's back and then put his hands on Nathan's hips, turning him for a quick kiss. "There you go."

"Thanks."

Owen kept out of the way as Nathan started frying the steaks, and his mouth watered as the delicious smell filled the kitchen. Nathan got a little flustered when everything seemed to be ready at the same time, and he finally let Owen help, giving him the job of draining the potatoes and stirring some butter into them ready to serve.

"Okay." Nathan wiped his brow. "This is all ready for me to serve up now. Can you take my wine through and top me up? I'll bring the food in a sec."

"Sure."

The steak was amazing. Exactly as Owen liked it, and he knew the noise of appreciation he made as he chewed on his first mouthful was slightly obscene. But he couldn't bring himself to care.

"Good, huh?" Nathan raised his eyebrows.

Owen just nodded, mouth full of food.

Nathan smiled and went back to eating.

They let their ankles tangle under the table as they ate, and whenever Owen let his gaze drift up to Nathan's face, Nathan seemed to be watching him. The wine and food were warm in Owen's belly, making him relaxed, and he let the good feeling of Nathan's company and attention wash over him and seep into his skin.

They finished the bottle of wine between them, but then switched to water by unspoken agreement. Owen didn't want his senses dulled for what he hoped would be happening later, and he definitely didn't want to get too sleepy.

"Have you got room for pudding?" Nathan asked when their plates were empty.

"Always." Owen grinned. "But maybe a small helping for now?"

"Okay. No... leave those. I'll take them. Back in a minute." Nathan refused Owen's offer of help again and disappeared into the kitchen with the plates.

Owen heard the rattle of the plates being set down and then the fridge door opening and closing. All was silent for a while till he heard Nathan cursing.

When Nathan reappeared with a bowl in each hand, his expression was rueful. "The stupid thing had stuck to the tin and it fell apart a little when I tried to dish it up. It looks a mess now."

"It'll taste the same." Owen shrugged. "What is it?" He peered into the bowls as Nathan lowered them.

"Lemon cheesecake with raspberry coulis."

"Oh my God. I love you."

Nathan faltered for a moment, his hand wobbling as he put Owen's bowl down, and a blush swept over Owen's face and neck as he realised what he'd said. Nathan recovered first, but his voice sounded a little strained as he replied, "Don't get carried away, it's only food."

"Yeah," Owen managed. He distracted himself from the awkwardness by digging his spoon in and having a taste. "Oh, wow, that's amazing." He risked a glance at Nathan and saw his cheeks were pink too. But he was smiling, so Owen relaxed a little.

They finished their pudding in silence. Owen's head was still turning over, unsettled by the words that had popped out of his mouth. It wasn't that he meant them—or he didn't think he did. It was too soon, surely. Could you really fall in love with someone in five weeks? Owen wasn't even sure he knew what love looked like. He hadn't grown up with a good example of it. But he knew Nathan was important to him, and when Owen was with him, it felt right and made Owen happy in a new kind of way that he'd never experienced before. He tried to squash his sudden onslaught of feelings into something more manageable but he still felt unsettled by the time they'd finished eating.

"Let me take these," Owen insisted. He stood and picked up Nathan's bowl as well as his own before Nathan could argue. Owen needed a break from the intensity of sitting opposite Nathan. Every time he caught Nathan's eye, it made his heart thump.

In the kitchen, Owen turned on the tap to rinse the plates and bowls. He couldn't see a dishwasher in the tiny kitchen, so guessed the dishes would need washing by hand. There was washing-up liquid on the windowsill over the sink, and Owen started to run some water, adding a blob of detergent and watching the bubbles froth and rise as the water poured in.

"You don't need to do that."

Firm hands on his hips made Owen jump. He hadn't heard Nathan come in over the sound of the water running.

"It's fine." Owen dumped the cutlery into the bowl. "You went to all this trouble. It's the least I can do."

Nathan pressed closer and kissed Owen's neck, sending a delicious shiver down his spine.

"I can think of other things you could do." Nathan whispered the words right by the shell of Owen's ear and ground the obvious bulge of his erection against Owen's arse. Owen's knees almost lurched as the weight of desire pooled in his belly and his dick stiffened in his jeans.

"Okay." He knew when he was beaten. "I like your plan better."

He turned in Nathan's arms and let Nathan push him up against the sink, kissing him slow and filthy until they were both panting and rubbing against each other a little desperately.

Owen finally broke away because the edge of the counter was sharp against his back. He grinned up at Nathan, who looked wrecked already, lips wet, and pink from Owen's stubble.

"Come on." He took Nathan's hand and led him towards the living room. "How about I blow you to show my appreciation for dinner?" He pushed Nathan down on the sofa and kicked his legs apart.

"Fuck." Nathan stared up at him with hunger in his eyes.

"Later maybe. This first."

Owen knelt, reaching for Nathan's fly. He unfastened the button and zip to reveal the gorgeous bulge of Nathan's cock through some obscenely tight briefs. He swallowed, mouth already watering with anticipation. But he didn't rush to get Nathan's cock out because he looked so hot like this, his erection straining against the thin fabric. Owen dipped his head and nuzzled the soft bulge of Nathan's balls, breathing in the scent of aroused man—*his* man, well... he hoped. He pushed that doubt aside for now, humming as Nathan tangled his fingers gently in Owen's hair and breathed his name.

He mouthed his way up the shaft to the head and licked, making Nathan gasp, cock flexing under Owen's tongue. But the fabric was too dry in Owen's mouth, and he wanted to taste, so he hooked his fingers in the elastic and lifted it, letting Nathan's cock spring free. Flushed with blood and already shiny and slick at the tip, it was as gorgeous as the man it was part of.

Without wasting any more time, Owen guided it into his mouth and lost himself in the slow slide of hot skin and the salty sweetness of Nathan on his tongue. Nathan stroked Owen's hair, his fingers tightening in the strands when Owen licked around the head.

Owen's own cock was rock hard from doing this for Nathan. He put a hand down to adjust himself, enjoying the pressure of his palm for a moment. But he wasn't in a hurry, so he kept his focus on pleasing Nathan, taking his time, and working him over till he was panting and moaning. Owen had one hand on Nathan's balls, teasing and stroking, and Nathan gasped as Owen let a finger slide back a little farther. But Nathan's trousers prevented him from reaching his target, so Owen pulled off for a moment.

"Up." He patted Nathan on the hip, eased his trousers and underwear down when Nathan lifted for him, and let them drop around Nathan's ankles. "That's better. Now shuffle down a bit."

Owen encouraged Nathan to slouch down so he could get better access to his arse, then went back to blowing him with a spit-slick finger circling his hole.

"Fuck, yes," Nathan muttered. "More."

Owen glanced up at Nathan's flushed face. He'd thrown his head back, and his hair was a mess from where Owen's hands had been in it while they were snogging in the kitchen. Nathan's eyes were closed, but as though he felt Owen looking, they flickered open, and he raised his head so their gazes locked.

"I want you to fuck me." Nathan's desperation made Owen's cock ache with the need to be inside him. But Nathan was so close, Owen didn't want to make him wait while he faffed around with lube and condoms. All his focus was on Nathan's pleasure right now.

He released Nathan's cock, stroking him with his free hand for a moment. "Later, yeah?"

"Yeah, okay." Nathan nodded, sliding his fingers into Owen's hair again as Owen lowered his head to take Nathan back into his mouth.

He sucked harder now, keeping up a rhythm that made his jaw ache. Nathan's hole relaxed against Owen's fingers, and he worked the tips inside, feeling Nathan clench and then release still further with a broken moan.

"Gonna come," Nathan warned. "Fuck, Owen!" His hips bucked, and Owen took him deep, tasting the hot rush of come as it filled his mouth. Owen carried on sucking, messy and slippery now, teasing at Nathan's rim with his fingers, gradually slowing down as he felt Nathan relax. The touch of Nathan's hands on his face made him stop and finally pull off and swallow.

"You're a mess." Nathan smiled. "C'mere."

He pulled on Owen's shoulders until Owen climbed into his lap for a kiss, and Nathan licked at the corner of Owen's mouth where some of his come had escaped before kissing him deeply. Owen kissed him back, lost in the sweetness of it. His heart felt swollen, still too full with feelings he didn't know what to do with. But he knew he wanted to try and communicate them to Nathan. He needed Nathan to know.

Nathan put a hand on the bulge of Owen's cock and squeezed, moving away from Owen's mouth to murmur against his neck, "Want me to suck you now? Or do you want to fuck me? You might need to give me a few minutes."

"Fuck. Yes... but I want to talk to you first. So a few minutes is fine."

"Talk?" Nathan sounded so stunned that Owen laughed.

"Yep... talk, communicate, interact. You're familiar with the concept, yes?" He moved off Nathan's lap but didn't go far. He sat beside him on the sofa, one hand on Nathan's bare thigh.

"Okay, let me just..." Nathan stood and pulled his trousers back up. "I can't have a serious conversation with my pants round my ankles. And you sound serious."

He frowned, and Owen wanted to chase away the look of anxiety on his face.

"I am. But it's good serious. Well—I hope it's good." Owen turned to meet Nathan's eyes and took a deep breath. "I'm just going to lay it all out there. This last five weeks have been amazing, and the reason I freaked out so badly last weekend when you said... what you said... is because I really like you. A lot. Honestly, at first I did see you as a conquest, and I didn't want to wait five weeks. It was a bit of a game at the beginning. But then I realised that I cared about you more than I wanted to fuck you."

Nathan raised a disbelieving eyebrow.

Owen clarified with a sheepish grin, "Okay, maybe not *more*. Because, God. Clearly I want to fuck you. You're gorgeous, and I've fancied you for years. But I want more than just a shag from you. I know this whole five-date challenge has been kind of contrived, not like a real relationship. But now the five dates are over — well, nearly over — I need you to know that five dates aren't enough." Owen throat was dry as he got the words out, and his voice cracked a little as he added, "And I want to carry on seeing you. If you're up for it."

Owen looked down at his hands where he had them twisted in his lap. There was a silence that felt endless, and Owen could hear every panicked beat of his heart as he waited.

"This is the part where you're supposed to say something." He knocked Nathan's knee with his own, too afraid to look at him.

When Nathan finally spoke, his voice was soft and husky. "Yeah, sorry. I don't know what to say…. I wasn't expecting such a declaration. But yes. Of course I'm bloody up for it."

Owen looked up, and the wonder and emotion on Nathan's face made his heart surge.

Nathan continued, "I've had a crush on you for years, too, but I never thought anything would come of it. Even when you agreed to date me, I didn't think it would work. I thought you'd get bored with me before five dates were up."

"Proved you wrong then, didn't I?" Owen gave him a small smile.

Nathan took his hand and laced their fingers together. "Yeah. Definitely." His face lit up with a grin. "So are you going to fuck me now? And there were promises of rimming during a certain phone call…."

"Hell, yes."

Nathan stood, pulling Owen up with him. "Well, what are we waiting for?"

"I have no idea."

Owen's arousal was a low, slow burn in the pit of his stomach as they undressed each other slowly. Hands caressing, lips touching and tasting. He felt as though he'd been hard for hours, but he desperately wanted to please Nathan. It was a new experience for Owen, putting somebody else's needs before his own. He found he liked it. Obviously with his previous conquests, he'd wanted to make sure they got off too, but he'd never wanted to revel in it before, to focus all his energy on the other person.

He spread Nathan out, face down on the sheets, and nuzzled between his cheeks, pressing soft kisses to the skin while Nathan squirmed beneath him. He pushed Nathan's thighs wider until he could see his pink hole in its nest of blond fuzz.

"Oh, yeah, you look so good. I wanna taste you. Is that okay?"

"Yeah." Nathan's voice sounded strained.

Owen grinned as he parted Nathan's cheeks and lowered his face to lick.

He started gently, teasing Nathan with barely there licks and kisses. Nathan was quiet, but Owen could feel the tension in his muscles and hear the rasp of his breath.

"You okay?" Owen pulled back to ask, stroking Nathan lightly with his fingertips instead for a moment. He wanted to be sure that Nathan was enjoying this if it was new to him.

"Yeah. It's good... really good," Nathan replied, his voice a little hoarse.

"I want to hear you, then."

Owen went back in, pressing harder with his tongue now, focusing right on Nathan's hole until any self-consciousness Nathan might have had was swept away by desperation and he started to moan and rock against Owen's face.

"Oh fuck, yeah... fuck. Please, Owen. *Fuck*."

Owen was almost tempted to let Nathan come like that, with Owen's tongue on his hole and a helping hand around his cock.

But then Nathan gasped out, "Oh God, Owen. It's so good, but I want you to fuck me. *Please*."

Owen wasn't going to say no to that, not this time.

"Hurry," Nathan grumbled as Owen rolled the condom on and made himself slick.

"This *is* me hurrying. Stop being bossy."

Owen smiled as Nathan huffed. Then he lay down and pulled Nathan onto his side so that Owen lay spooned up behind him. His cock nudged the backs of Nathan's thighs as Owen pushed carefully into him with a couple of lubey fingers, smearing it around. "Need me to stretch you more or are we good?"

"We're good. Just do it."

So Owen did.

He bent Nathan's upper leg and lifted it a little, positioned himself and then pressed inside carefully, feeling the give of the muscle as Nathan's body drew him in.

It was Owen's turn to gasp now. "Jesus, Nathan. Feels so good."

Owen fucked him slowly at first, holding back, edging himself. When he felt like he was getting too close, he paused to focus on kissing Nathan's shoulders and stroking his cock. But soon Nathan was urging him on, pushing back into every thrust, trying to make Owen go faster.

"I'm really close." Nathan wrapped his hand around Owen's where it was on his cock, squeezing more tightly and guiding the movement. "Yeah, like that…. Fuck me harder. God, *yes*."

Nathan groaned, come spurting over their linked fingers. His internal muscles pulsed around Owen, dragging him over the edge till he came too, his cries muffled by the hot skin of Nathan's shoulder as he bucked into him, pulsing out his orgasm until he was spent.

After, they lay locked together, sweaty skin on skin, their hands still clasped around Nathan's softening dick. Owen kissed Nathan's shoulders and back — sweet, gentle kisses as his heart gradually slowed.

"God," Nathan sighed.

"Yeah, that was…." Owen couldn't find the words.

Nathan shifted, looking over his shoulder so Owen could reach his mouth in an awkward kiss.

"Hang on." Owen eased out carefully and sorted out the condom, tossing it on the floor. Nathan rolled onto his back and watched him, then pulled Owen into his arms when he was done. They pulled the duvet up to their waists and lay wrapped around each other.

Owen felt dazed, full of an intense happiness that was new to him. Nathan's heart thudded softly in his ear, and Owen felt as though his was being pulled into time with it, aligning their beats until they sounded as one.

"Do you think it's possible to fall in love with someone in five weeks?" he asked.

Nathan huffed in a sharp intake of breath, and his hand tightened on Owen's shoulder where he was holding him. When he replied his voice was rough.

"I should bloody hope so, because I knew after three."

Owen's chest tightened, and something that felt alarmingly like tears prickled his eyelids. He blinked hurriedly. "Really?"

"Mm-hmm." A deep rumble in Nathan's chest.

192

"So. Five more dates, then?" Owen tried to keep his tone light, but it came out a little strangled.

"I don't know. I'm not sure five will be enough."

"Fifty, then?"

"That sounds better," Nathan replied. "Although if we're still only having Saturday as official date night, that's nearly a whole year you'd have to put up with me."

"I think I can live with that." Owen tipped his head back so he could see the smile on Nathan's face. "But we are allowed sex on the dates from now on, just to be clear?"

Nathan laughed. "Hell, yes."

About the Author

Jay lives just outside Bristol in the West of England, with her husband, two children, and two cats. Jay comes from a family of writers, but she always used to believe that the gene for fiction writing had passed her by. She spent years only ever writing emails, articles, or website content.

One day, she decided to try and write a short story–just to see if she could–and found it rather addictive. She hasn't stopped writing since.

www.jaynorthcote.com
Twitter: @jay_northcote
Email: jaynorthcote@gmail.com

Also by Jay Northcote

Nothing Serious
The Little Things
Coming Home
Not Just Friends
Nothing Special

Coming Soon

Nothing Ventured

10586222R00116

Printed in Great Britain
by Amazon.co.uk, Ltd.,
Marston Gate.